The Creatures at the Absolute Bottom of the Sea

# THE CREATURES AT
# THE ABSOLUTE BOTTOM
# OF THE SEA

*Rosemary McGuire*

University of Alaska Press: Fairbanks

© University of Alaska Press
P.O. Box 756240
Fairbanks, AK 99775-6240

Cover photo by Thomas Desvignes

Library of Congress Cataloging-in-Publication Data
McGuire, Rosemary Desideria.
[Short stories. Selections]
The creatures at the absolute bottom of the sea : stories / Rosemary McGuire.
pages cm
ISBN 978-1-60223-259-4 (pbk. : alk. paper) — ISBN 978-1-60223-260-0 (electronic)
1. Fishers—Fiction. 2. Alaska--Fiction. I. Title. II. Title: Creatures at the absolute
bottom of the sea.
PS3613.C4996A6 2015
813'.6—dc23
2014023213

*For Ted*

# CONTENTS

# ACKNOWLEDGMENTS

I would like to thank Thomas & Sally McGuire, Frank Soos, Peggy Shumaker, and James Engelhardt for all the help and time they've given me.

I would also like to thank the fishermen and -women I've worked with all these years for allowing me to listen to their stories.

# PROLOGUE

*Togiak, May*

We're anchored in the Naknek River, waiting. The river slides by in darkness, the sound of water slapping against the hull. In the cabin, a single light burns, and under it we sit around the table. The boat is to be taken out of the water in the morning.

The men's shoulders cast shadows over my page. They're talking. Mark draws a map for Nate, showing him fishing grounds he's learned in twenty years of work. Nate nods, stabbing his finger down on the map. "So, this is . . ." He's impatient for knowledge, eager to get to his boat and take it out on his own first opener. To him, fishing is new and exciting, not an old story of bills and breakdowns. Though he sympathizes with Mark, he can't share his pain.

Mark keeps talking. They pass the whiskey back and forth. Drunk now, Nate assures us, "I am a badass," in complete sincerity. Every time he goes out on deck to piss, Mark and I follow to make sure he doesn't fall overboard. Now both of them are telling stories. I can't shout loud enough to be heard, so I bend my head to my notebook, listen, and write.

When the stories slow, I see tears trembling in Mark's eyes, ready to fall. There is no way to escape or fathom this sadness. This is our real life.

The Creatures at the Absolute Bottom of the Sea

# THE LOST BOYS LONGLINE CO.

Four boys walked in single file down the steel ramp into the harbor. Corey followed Billy, followed Bob who followed Jack past the stand with last year's newspaper still unchanged, the sheds of longline gear and someone's gill net lying ice caked and covered in yellow snow, to the *Alrenice* where she lay on the farthest float.

"What do people eat?" Corey asked. He was the cook because he was the least experienced, and because he seemed no use for anything else. Corey'd drifted into Thompsen's Bay a season before, but so far no one felt inclined to think of him as part of the town.

"I dunno. Oreos?" Billy said. "I like 'em."

"I'll give you a grocery list," Jack said absently. He was twenty, the oldest, and skipper of the boat. "Hamburger. More hamburger. Onions and stuff. I'll write it down."

"Thanks," Corey said. He smiled up at Jack, hoping too obviously to be liked.

"We'll need more oil, too. Oil rags. Steering fluid. Fuel filters." Jack recited more important things, half to himself. The vein on his forehead throbbed, swollen. His thoughts strayed with nervousness. This was his first season running a boat for longlining, and he was afraid. Longline derbies were a crazy fishery. Twenty-four hours in the Gulf of Alaska to fish as hard as you could, and that was all you got. When the derby began, people had to fish no matter what the weather was like, and that was what made it dangerous. That, and the hurry and the tiredness from so many hours working without a break. And his crew was so damn young.

Alongside him, Billy and Bob wrestled like puppies, trying to trip each other into the water that slapped brackish against the creosote dock. The sun came out, half overcast, and lit up the harbor like a memory, briefly gilding the fishing boats. Jack glanced up at its position. Almost five o'clock.

"When we get down there, I'm going to do a couple things in the engine room before we take off," Jack said, deepening his voice. "I want you two to clean out the fish hold. Get the bin boards set up so we can go get ice. Corey, get the galley squared away. It looks like a goddamn lair in there. And scrub the stove. We don't want any botulism on board."

Corey looked at him, trusting him, and nodded. He didn't know that cleaning the galley was a low-status job, or that he was expected to bitch about it. Well, that was fine. When Jack went in the galley later to scrub oil off his hands, the stove was clean enough, and Corey was reading a cookbook he'd gotten at the library. One of the fund-raising kind with recipes by locals.

"Deckhand's Delight," Corey read out loud. "Quick 'n' Easy Hash 'n' Eggs. You want that for dinner, Jack?"

"Whatever," Jack said. "You can start cooking once we get under way." He sat down and double-checked the weather and tide. Twelve feet of water moving on the ebb. That would carry them swiftly out as far as Hinchinbrook at least, and save on fuel. Winds variable ten tonight, with patchy fog. Tomorrow a low was moving in, but it didn't sound bad.

He looked up again to check the time, then went down in the engine room and started the boat. Let her warm up a little. When the crew got back, they would take off.

≈ ≈ ≈

Dusk fell as they headed out, the quick dusk of early spring. Light had left the water, though it held the snow-piled peaks of higher ground. Overhead, the pale sky was streaked with the clouds people called mare's tails. The sea, darkening, held its perennial gravitas. It drew them out south and to the west, into gathering clouds. On their bow, a group of porpoises rode the wake, white sides flashing as they rolled and turned. Playing. Jack watched them as he steered. Trying not to think about the crew. Corey'd drifted off up the dock, again, just as they were ready to untie. It took half an hour to find him, get him back. But Jack couldn't bring himself to bitch him out.

In the galley now, Corey chopped an onion clumsily but with determination, his thin shoulders hunched inside his sweatshirt. His mild blue eyes shied up at Jack, full of their infuriating hopefulness. "This OK?" he said.

He knew he was in trouble, but he couldn't help it. Behind him, a pot of noodles simmered on the stove. When the food was ready, he set it on the table with a serving spoon and a stack of paper plates. It wasn't good, but it was hot and belly filling. The boys ate fast, faces down over their plates. When they finished, Jack told them to hit the rack.

"We'll be working early," he said.

"Want me to take a wheel watch?" Billy offered.

"No," Jack said. They crawled into their bunks in the forepeak, leaving him alone. Soon, he heard a double rhythm of snores, broken by the sound of the gathering swell and the wakes of other boats cutting over it. Most of the fleet had left on the same tide. One by one, the ships' captains passed him. Some waved. Others did not. His buddy George came too close on purpose, to make his wake smack into them and make them roll. Plates and cards slid on the table, almost fell. The guys shouldn't've left them there.

"Goddamn it!"

He could see George through the cabin window, grinning hard.

"Get a real boat," George's deckhand yelled. Jack flipped him off. The *Alrenice* was a fine boat, just a little old. He'd had a hard time finding anything to lease. A lot of guys were running boats by the time they were his age, and if their dads were good fishermen, they did well. They had the gear and experience, and they had access to a kind of unspoken system of fishermen helping one another—giving them tips for their dads' sakes, lending them a wrench or a hand when they needed it. But Jack's dad, Ronnie, was a worthless drunk, who couldn't even get his boat out to the grounds half the time. People joked that they crossed the street when they saw Ron coming, but it wasn't a joke. When Jack had leased the *Alrenice* last season, people said he'd sink it for sure. But he'd done all right seining in the Sound, and in the fall John Ross at the cannery even said, "You're not much like your old man."

Maybe he was lucky, he thought. His dad never had been. Luck was a thing that adhered to a person, regardless of virtue; and though it could not be attracted, it could be driven off. Yes, he'd been lucky so far. He stroked the steering wheel of his boat, his own boat. By himself, he'd installed her new hydraulics when the old ones went. He'd been there when they put this engine in. She was his, though he only leased her.

Hopefulness. The hopefulness and love. Darkness fell now. Ahead, the moon rose over the starboard bow, and higher up, the long bright arc of the Big Dipper. He'd write a poem about it if he knew the words.

Below him, Corey stirred. "Everything all right?" he asked, leaning out of his bunk, helpful and strangely helpless at the same time. The other two still snored.

"Yeah. You lay down. I'll get you up if I need you," Jack said. He was filled with a kind of warm feeling. He wanted to share it; and at the same time, he wanted to be alone. "You did good today," he told Corey expansively. The boy smiled. It wasn't his fault he was a klutz.

Silence and darkness crept in once more.

≈ ≈ ≈

Past Hinchinbrook, they got into ocean swell and the pure, deep waters of the Gulf. The tide began to turn, and the boat slowed. At 3:00 a.m., Jack got Billy up.

"Just keep her as she is," he told him. "We're heading pretty much straight south now." Before he crawled in his bunk, he went out on the deck for a last look around. The land had fallen far behind them. All he could see was a faint, dark mass somewhere on the horizon, against the clear, black depth of the sky. Stars swung high overhead. Northern lights, maybe the last of the year. Standing there, he felt exhilaration as cold and deep as water. It seemed to drive into him out of the night. He was Jack. He was alive. This was his boat. His crew, and he was young. How strange the sea was. Like a god, but he himself was like a god. His thoughts fumbled, exalted, and his body shook with a physical fear and heat.

When he woke again, they were within ten miles of the fishing grounds. A light wind had come up with the dawn. It was overcast. Outside, steel gray water surged and tumbled, stretching out to the horizon in a monotonous wasteland. There was the taste of metal in his mouth. He got the boys up and made a pot of coffee. Billy put a box of Snickers between them on the table.

"Breakfast," he said. They were still half awake, their eyes sleep fogged. Hair tousled upright on their heads, their faces red and crumpled with the weight of dreams. Billy had the mark of a zipper imprinted on his forehead like a scar. He'd used his jacket for a pillow.

"All right," Jack said. "Let's get the deck set up." He knew it was early yet. But he wanted the guys to look at it, to stand on deck for a while as if they could absorb the knowledge that would make them a decent crew by simple proximity to water and gear. Billy, he knew, had crewed in a longline derby before. Bob had not, but he had experience on boats, and he'd pick it up quickly. They'd handle the deck. Corey would help out where he could, and he himself would run the boat from the steering station on top of the house.

"A'ight," Bob said, drawling to be funny. They were fired up now. Excited. Energy crackled from them. They dragged their gear on and went out. Jack followed them, pushing open a hatch so that he could see the instruments from overhead. He climbed the ladder onto the top of the house and took control at the steering station there. A light drizzle began to fall, cutting visibility. Three boats waited to the south of them. There'd be many others in the fog.

Billy hooked a line anchor to the first tub of gear. Behind him, more tubs waited, the long ground lines coiled and ready, baited hooks arranged along the rim. Along the cabin, Bob hung the gaffs, to be ready when they brought the lines back in.

Jack glanced down and checked the time again. 7:55. One of the other boats had crowded in. On deck, he could see the crew at work, their bright orange rain gear glowing through the drizzling mist. "Fuckers," he said, quietly, nervously. They idled past. Downwind, the other two boats drifted as they waited.

7:59. "Get ready," he called, and watched as the second hand steadily traced the blurred face of the clock.

"All right," he called as it touched the twelve. Eight o'clock. He threw the *Alrenice* in gear. Billy heaved the line anchor overboard. The line peeled out over the stern, hooks flying, each tied on a gangion and baited with herring. When the line ran out, Billy whipped another tub in place. They kept on setting. Off to his side, the other boat was setting—too close to him, he thought, as if it was a challenge. "Fuck," he said. His world had narrowed to the deck below, the hooks flashing overboard, and the course before him. The other boat was a threat, nothing more; competition for the fish that lay below. Neck and neck they raced, and the hooks flew out to settle down into the cold depth of the water. Two thousand feet here.

"All right, that's good," Jack called. He'd set the next string in a different depth. The boys let the line whip out, buoyed it, and stood, motion arrested, waiting for the next set. He ran a few moments, watching the sounder.

"Let 'er rip," he called. Again Billy chucked the anchor and the line went out. They finished setting and ran south again to lay the next string.

Halfway through the morning, the wind began coming up. Jack watched it, worrying. It might take a long time for them to pick up if it started to blow. But it was hard to quit. An hour passed before he turned north again, back to where they'd started laying out.

"Fuck," he said again. He'd forgotten to write down the loran coordinates for the first string. He ran now, searching for it in the fog. When he saw it, he yelled.

"Corey. In the hold. You're packing the fish in ice. Bob—you gut 'em. Billy gaffs." Billy hooked the buoy and brought it aboard. The line came in over the power block and spooled messily into the tubs. Bait chunks still clung to it, water-sodden. Billy gaffed each fish as it broke the surface, yanked it aboard, and threw it to Bob at the cutting table. Bob gutted it and threw it down to Corey in the hold, to be packed in ice. The fishing was fair. Too many green eyes and trash fish, though, not enough of the lovely black cod that brought such high-dollar prices from the Japanese. But the wind was still coming up. It was hard to work on the pitching deck.

As the dark came down, Jack saw his crew moving wearily. He kicked the deck lights on, illuminating them with a hard, stark light. Cranked the music louder. Black Sabbath. The bass-line beat under the deck vibrated, and his chest began to choke up and pound with the music. "Generals gather in their masses," Corey sang from the hold in a scratchy voice. "Just like witches at black masses . . ." His voice broke on the last note. The music drugged them, driving back their weariness.

It had begun to blow in earnest now. Wind whipped the water into chop, and the chop built into larger waves that surged past them, their white crests moving through the dark. The *Alrenice* settled into them, riding the trough. As each crest came, the wind struck her with redoubled force. Overhead the stars had disappeared. Rain came spitting down. Jack pulled his hood up, then pushed it back. He needed to be able to see, to keep her with her stern into the seas. His hands were icy. Down on deck the guys worked like machines. Gaff. Toss. Gut. Toss. Pack. Pack. Once Bob lost his balance and fell to the deck, sidestepping Corey, who was in the wrong place again and out of the hold for no good reason. Jack felt the familiar baffled mixture of frustration and protectiveness rise in his throat. How could the kid be so dumb? But Bob was too numb even to be angry. He was up again and gutting before anyone could react, and Bill thrust Corey back toward the hold, no harder than he needed to.

They finished that string. "All right," Jack called. He looked down at his scrawled list, taped to the wall under the partial shelter of the console, for the next coordinates. East northeast of here. He turned the boat. Billy left the deck and came to stand beside him. "What's the forecast, Skip?" he said, trying to grin.

"Shitty. I listened to the update 'bout an hour ago. It's supposed to blow sixty, but not before tomorrow night. We should be back in town by then."

Billy bit his lip and looked out at the water. "Think it's coming early? Seems like it's picking up pretty damn quick."

"Yeah. I dunno. Maybe." Jack turned slightly, to indicate he didn't want to talk. "We're coming up on her now," he said. Billy went back down on deck. Jack peered into the dark. Where in the fuck was that bloody buoy? You couldn't even see it in the dark, much less in the troughs of the waves. "What I'd give for a radar." For forty minutes, he combed the area before giving up. Maybe the buoy'd broken loose. It happened. He looked down, memorized the next coordinates, and turned again. Fuck, that was a lot of money to lose. He'd'a paid for the radar right there, with that lost string. But the trouble with that kind of thinking was you couldn't get the money in advance. And all that they might catch today was already spent on payments and gasoline and bait.

"Bloody hell," he yelled suddenly into the wind.

"You call?" Bob shouted.

"No," he said. This wind was like an enemy. It tumbled them, playing the way a cat might play a mouse. And they would lose in the end. No one had ever outlived the water; and the water had never cared about anybody, and never would. It didn't even know. That was the thing. There was no one to know. The sea just was. It wasn't anybody.

He looked back at the deck. The guys had hunched down out of the wind. He looked forward again, and there was his buoy, marked in lavender stripes, the only color not in use when he bought his pots.

"Comin' up on her," he yelled. Billy jumped up, obedient, to hook the buoy.

By 1:00 a.m., it was gusting sixty knots. They finished picking up the last string and went back to search again for the one they'd lost. He combed the water for an hour but never found it. Most of the boats were already heading in, running from the weather. The fishing wasn't good enough to risk lives. He looked out at the darkness and shivered.

"A'ight," he called. "We're heading in." Corey crawled out of the hold. The boys secured the deck and crowded into the cabin. When he saw the last of them off deck, he ran to follow and grabbed the steering wheel inside the house. The weather seemed a little better from in here. The *Alrenice* could handle seas like these. It was the cold that had gotten to him, and the black water behind him, below the edge of the boat.

"Fuck," he said. "Was getting a little nasty out there."

"Hell, yeah," Bob said. "How well d'you think we did?"

"Maybe two thousand pounds." He shrugged. They wouldn't really know until they got back to town and heard how much the other boats had caught. That was what mattered, more than anything. But if the price was good, two thousand pounds was a fair bit of money. He could see his crew furrow their brows as they tried to work out what their shares would be. He'd never known a deckhand so dumb that he couldn't work percentages and calculate his pay accurately.

"Not bad," Bob said, through a mouthful of grub. He had a can of chili in one hand and a box of Toll House cookies in the other. "Jesus," he said. "My hands smell so bad; I can't hardly eat with 'em. Smell like bait," he said. He held them up, still seamed and red with cold, and tried to flex his fingers. "Son of a bitch, I can't make a fist. Skipper, skipper, I want disability," he said.

"Disability my ass," Jack said. "You can't make a fist because you're weak. I should dock your pay." He spoke half absently, joshing him out of habit without looking around.

"You guys want to hit the rack, you can," he said. "I'm going to steer at least until we get in behind the islands. If I start to fall asleep, I'll get one of you up to talk to me."

"'Kay," Bob said. He stood, kicked off his boots, and crawled, still in his jacket, into his bunk. The others followed. Reaching up, Jack set the watch alarm for thirty seconds and sat punching it repetitively to keep awake. If his eyes closed, if he quit hitting that button, the alarm would sound and wake him before they fell off course.

Jesus, it was a long way home. He couldn't even see another boat.

Maybe they were still fishing. Or maybe they were all ahead of him, in behind the islands, safe. The VHF emitted a soft drone of static, broken now and then by the sound of someone speaking, too far off to be picked up. But they were only an hour from Hinchinbrook. Back there, he could rest a while.

His head began to bow over the wheel, while his raised arm kept punching the button of the watch alarm. He steered almost in a dream. It seemed to him someone was warning him—of what he did not know. Ahead, the waves rolled steadily on. He kept the course, kept his swollen eyes on the water, as his mind began to sink from him. Someone was warning him. Of what? There were green fields. And suddenly, he felt a kind of peace, as if the worst was already over, and passed or not, he'd never face that test again.

He wakened from his half sleep to the sound of the bilge alarm. It sounded once, went off, and sounded again. Already, he was on his feet.

"Get up, guys," he shouted. They stumbled out of their bunks, pale faces sleepy and alarmed. "Bill, you steer. I'm going to check the engine room. Bob, you come with me, make sure I don't fall overboard. Corey, stand by." He grabbed a flashlight and pushed the door open. The boat was rolling so hard the scuppers were awash. He could see nothing but blackness. On the back deck, he and Bob kicked open the freeman hatch to the engine room and yanked it up. Nothing.

Thoughts went through his mind in hurried, random order. He stood up.

"Hatch back," he shouted at Bob over the sound of the wind. They heaved it back and clamped it down. He ran for the stern and clawed at the hatch to the lazarette, tearing his knuckles open as he lifted it back. Below them, he saw two feet of water in the hold, sliding murderously with the motion of the boat. "Son of a bitch," he whispered.

Maybe it was just her seams working in the weather. Or maybe some of the packing had slipped out, and in that case they might be fucked. "Bob. There's a spare pump under the portside bench in the galley. Get that. Coil of wire in the bottom drawer. Get that, too.

Run." He jumped into the lazarette, groped in cold water for the bilge pump, hauled it out, and checked for a loose connection. It seemed to work. He dropped it back in again, jumped out, and snatched the spare from Bob's hand as he hustled over the deck. Grabbing the coil of wire, he ran back into the cabin, hooked it to the batteries, and spooled it out through the cabin door, all the way across the deck to the lazarette. He clamped on the spare pump and threw it in the laz.

"Where's the bloody hand pump?" he shouted. Bob ran for it. Jack grabbed it from his hands, thrust it into the lazarette. "Get down in there, and do what you can with that." Bob scrambled in, gasping as the cold water struck him, and began to pump.

There wasn't much room in the laz. Jack squeezed past him under the deck, looking for the leak with a flashlight. Water was seeping in from many seams, but he could not find a major source. There must be one. It must already be underwater, he thought. How the fuck do you find a leak underwater?

"Faster," he yelled at Bob. "Fucking faster." Bob hunched over, his arm pistoning in the shadows cast by the flashlight. The water crept higher up his legs. Jack scrabbled under water for the pumps and checked them both. Still working. "Fuck!"

Corey's face bent over the lazarette. Jack yelled, "Get some bedding. Sweatshirts. Anything!"

"What?"

"I said, get your fucking bedding." Corey's face disappeared, a look of incomprehension pasted across it. Jack knelt down in the water, now waist deep, and felt the seams of his boat with his hand. If he could just find where she was leaking. If he could get something in it, plug it with clothes. He was working now by instinct. It seemed to him he ought to be able to feel in his own body where his boat was damaged, as he would feel a breach of the barrier of his skin and an outpouring of his blood. He reacted as one reacts in fistfight, looking for an opening and not falling, even though the fight was all but done.

Corey's face reappeared above the hatch, his arms laden with sleeping bags. "This what you want?"

Jack grabbed one from him, and began tamping it into the seam along her keel. It blew out again. He felt the water rushing through his fingers and slid them up into a wide crack. He tamped the fabric back. But it would not stay. The water was chest deep now. It lapped, cold and salty, against his face as he knelt, slid into his clenched, resisting mouth. He shut his eyes and ducked below the surface, feeling once more for the breach. But it was too late.

"Get your survival suits on and get back out on deck," he said. "We're sinking." Bob dropped the pump and vaulted heavily from the lazarette with the speed of one released from a death trap. Corey beat him to the cabin door and dragged the survival suits from the forepeak. He thrust one at each of the men. They tore them open and struggled into them. Heavy, orange insulating foam, zipped up to the neck. Not all the boats had them, but they did. Billy's zipper jammed near his throat. He was a heavy kid, and his sweatshirt hood kept him from getting the survival suit over his head. He struggled with it. Corey tried to help.

"Jesus Christ," Jack yelled behind them. "Get out on deck. If this thing rolls . . ." If it rolled, they would be trapped inside. He grabbed the mike. "Mayday, Mayday," he said. "This is the *Alrenice*." Fumbling with the chart, he gave their latitude and longitude. "We're taking on water. Mayday."

The radio spat static. Dimly he heard the Coast Guard station in Kodiak come back to him, "Vessel *Alrenice*, do you copy?"

"I copy you," he said, but the boat gave a sickening lurch. Slowly, as the water in her shifted, she went over, settling as she went. The lights went dead, and the radio. He dropped the mike and ran for the deck, kicking his legs into his suit as he fled. Outside, the boys were clinging to the house. The *Alrenice* lay half on her side, still partly afloat. The skates of longline gear had broken loose, and the deck was awash with lines and hooks.

"Life . . . raft . . ." Jack shouted, scrambling up the side of the house. Billy followed him. They got the life raft out, but as it inflated, the wind caught it and it blew away. It skated lightly over the surface. He felt the water slide again, and the boat move with it, sullenly. He thought she would sink then, but she still lay on her side, sideways to the ocean swell. He ran down onto the deck again, but he did not believe now that he could save his crew. Without the life raft, how could they make it through the night?

He grabbed a length of line and tried to drag it free from the tangle of longline snarled on the deck, thinking he would lash the four of them together. Another crest passed. The boat lurched, and he fell to his knees, gashing his hands and face on the bloody hooks. Or, better yet, he'd swim for the raft with a lifeline. He threw one end of it into Billy's hands.

"Hang on to that."

Behind him, Corey stared out at the bobbing raft. Suddenly he understood. He did not have a quick mind for things like this—the physical details of an event—but he saw his moment. He grabbed Jack by the arm. "I'll swim for it," he yelled. "I'm a stronger swimmer." It was true. It was the one thing he could do.

For a split second, Jack hesitated. Their eyes met. He nodded. Go. He knew it was safer to stay together. There was so little chance of finding a single man adrift in this sea. But they needed the raft. He didn't think they would survive without it. And though he couldn't ever have named the thought, he knew it had to be Corey, not one of his own.

"All right. Here," he shouted. He lashed the line to Corey's waist. "Go. I'll get you back." Corey stumbled overboard, into water full of floating gear. He swam clumsily, hampered by the suit. The life raft danced before him. On deck, the men saw him briefly, rising up the side of the waves, then sinking away.

The *Alrenice* settled again below them. She moved sluggishly, sideslipped, and sank beneath their feet. Jack grabbed for Corey's line, but it slipped away, plucked from his grasp by the weight of the boat falling. The line caught somewhere in the dark, where it might hold or free itself, but anyway all too far out of his desperate reach, and all promises were incomplete and done.

Then she was gone, and so was he. His mind went blank as the rush of water sucked him in, crushing him.

He found himself on the surface again, floating on water choked with tangled gear. The other boys were thrashing their way free. He could see their white faces in the dark.

"Keep together," he shouted. When he reached them, he grabbed Billy's arm. "Anybody see Corey?" His words rang empty.

Bob shook his head.

Jack clutched his arm to keep him close. With his other hand, he held Billy's shoulder. The water poured through the gashes in his survival suit. How long was it 'til morning? Four hours? Five?

"Hang on to me," he said. His limbs were already growing numb. Somehow, Bob managed to hold him tighter, so that he felt the pressure even through cold flesh. "Keep hanging on. Billy, hang on."

"OK," Bob said. "Take it easy, Skipper."

At dawn, they were picked up by the *Emma Ray*. Jack was half comatose by then. The boys still hung onto his arms. They scanned the surface, watching for Corey as Jack would scan it for the rest of his life, wondering still how things would have happened if that night he'd made some different choice, wondering what indeed he should have done. Though four months later, they found Corey's body, still in its survival suit, washed up on the shores of Kodiak.

*So that's all there was*, Jack thought when he heard the news. *A body. Flesh. And I dare you to find a reason for it all.*

He pushed the knowledge back. Tried not to think of all the things that Corey would never now know, the things that are done and undone, good and evil, and the days that cannot be recovered.

# THE MURDER

Mike came into the bar and put his hat down on the table between our glasses. He took a chair and straddled it.

"What's new?" he said.

I didn't answer.

After a moment, Bob said something. I looked out the window so as not to talk. Sunlight lay in blocks on the dusty carpet. The air smelled of fries and something more, the staleness of people sitting for too long. Outside, in the commercial harbor, boats lay heavily at the dock, rocking to the wake of a passing scow.

He reached across the table and punched my arm. "Bet you wished you was still working for me, didn't you?"

"No," I said. "I didn't wish that at all."

≈ ≈ ≈

Last August I was by the Dumpster, throwing out trash after longlining, when a truck pulled up. Carl Black leaned out. "Have you heard about the *St. John*?" he said.

"What about it?" I said.

"It's tied up at the dock in Valdez. Yellow tape all over it," he said. "I hear they tried to kill the skipper."

I nodded, but he kept on anyway.

"Last night one of Mike's deckhands finally snapped. That big kid, about twenty-one?"

"Yeah? What happened?"

"He tried to kill Mike with a marlinspike. Stabbed him three times in the chest.

"They said he was crazy," Carl said. "They took him to Anchorage. Big kid in handcuffs. I saw them drive away." His eyes looked shiny, wet with excitement.

On the other side of the Dumpster, Bill spoke up. "I'm on pins and needles," he said, in a voice like he'd been licking ashtrays. "Pins and needles. Tell me Mike died."

"You couldn't kill that bastard with a meat axe."

≈ ≈ ≈

I met Mike out in the Aleutians, not long after I got back from Iraq. Way out west there's nothing but a few ships, red and blue, so big they looked distorted, and the cranes on shore, loading and unloading stacks of ATCO units full of gear. The mountains looked high and bare, scoured by the wind and covered in snow as thick as cream. Past that lay the glassy, icy Bering Sea.

When I got off the plane from Anchorage, I walked down the road to the bar. It was New Year's Eve, but I was the only customer. The bartender was stringing paper signs and setting up like people might come in later. But the place had a tired, smelly air, and I knew that whatever I pretended, nothing good was apt to happen there.

All the same, I asked for a whiskey Coke. The bartender poured it small in a too-large glass.

"Ever been out here before?" he said.

"Nope," I said. "I grew up in Wasilla."

"That's a shit hole," he said.

I nodded. "Yeah. Palins and punks."

"Yeah," he said. "You fish?"

"I have," I said. "I'm looking for a job."

He glanced at me, at the jarhead haircut half grown out, the heft and height. I looked away from him, at the wall. He went back to stringing paper streamers, an old man, moving slow. His head had a kind of permanent dip, like he was bowing to me over and over. I watched him and I wondered what kind of bad luck makes you end up here, decorating an empty bar on New Year's Eve.

"You back home, soldier?" he said after a while.

"Yeah," I said.

"Looking for work?"

"Yeah."

"And fishing?" he repeated.

"I used to do it."

He looked back over his shoulder at me, and I knew what he was thinking. He nodded. Then suddenly it seemed like he was gone. Nothing was left but the husk of a man, bowing to the rows of bottle glass. That happened. Sometimes, nobody was real. And at other times, they were much too much like me. I couldn't tell where I stopped and they began.

I curled myself around my drink and waited.

After a time, another man came in. He spoke to the barman briefly and walked up to me.

"My name's Mike," he said. "You the guy looking for a job?"

"Yeah," I said. I shook his hand. "I'm Hank," I said. He was shorter than I expected, once I stood up. His eyes flat blue, too close together to quite meet mine. He looked at me hard. I looked back. His face seemed blurry in the aftermath of war.

I followed him out the door with my gear, past the canneries, and down onto the dock. I needed that job.

Down on the boat, a generator throbbed. Water sluiced across the deck from the hold where the reefer system was circ'ing a load of cod.

"We're running 'em to King Cove," Mike said. "Can't take 'em here."

I nodded. He undogged the galley door. Inside, two others sat at the table, Carhartt hats pulled low over their heads. A young guy hunched by the oil drip stove and an older man playing double solitaire. They glanced at me, their faces tired, eyes red rimmed and suspicious.

"This is Hank," Mike said to them. "Just so's you know. We'll be heading out in about a half hour." He walked me past the table to the fo'c'sle. It was down on level with the engine room. The door between them hadn't closed, and a film of dark grease lay spilled across the floor. Down there, the gen-set sounded even louder. Mike shook my arm and shouted over the din.

"Go ahead and move anything you want out of your bunk. Just find somewhere to chuck it."

I took a top bunk, pulled some tools out of it and stacks of gear. Put my duffel in and went upstairs. I was changing into my boots when the engine fired. Footsteps thudded and lines slapped on the deck. When I looked out, we were leaving the harbor mouth. Mike had gone. The others were coming in again, taking off their gear. They pushed aside their plates from dinner. One spun the cards together, dealing out rummy.

"Hey," I said.

The kid nodded, looking up. "Hey," he said.

I thought that they would cut me in. But the older man picked up the cards slowly, indifferently. Tapped the pack and put it away. He and the kid stood up, too beat to talk. I'd seen that look on faces in the war. I watched them walk down to the fo'c'sle. After a while, I got up, scraped their plates into the trash, and stood looking out the galley window at the swells that heaved unresolved past the boat and the dark bulk of the land falling in our wake.

The boat felt sour to me. I'd heard you can tell when a boat has a ghost, when someone died there, but this was the first time I'd felt that way myself. The air was electric with things gone wrong. Things I didn't know. Then I told myself I was just scatty. I had to get used to living here again, not to feel all the time as if I were under attack.

I stared out the porthole at the surface, and then I realized I'd let the water run down the sink as if there was no end to it, though I didn't even know how much we had. Guiltily, I shut off the tap and stood, hands hanging loose, not knowing where to go or what to do. I felt these blanknesses inside me sometimes. I could go so far down; I could lose myself in a space in my mind that had always been there, a place without language or time. I wondered if everyone had that, if we were all part of an archipelago of private silences that would not connect. But if you went further, were they all the same? And did the other men do that, too?

I caught myself thinking too hard and shook my head to free myself from me. Then I wondered if this was a bad-luck boat. Later, I knew it was so.

The vessel itself was in rough shape. Once I went down in the engine room with a hammer and chisel. I thought if I could pound that chisel through the bottom, I was finished. But I must've picked the only sound piece of steel in the whole fucking bottom, because it wouldn't go through. And I sat there looking at the bilge, the sheets of waste steel peeling off the fiddly and falling in scales of powdered rust. The water sliding down the walls, and the lights that slipped off the greasy floor. The pipes snaked around the room and walled me in.

But it was more than just the boat. Mike was afraid of us. He kept a pistol by his bunk. I saw it that night when he called me up to the wheelhouse to show me how to steer. He kept it loaded, ready to fire.

*It's not a ghost,* I thought. These men had just been here too long. I could smell it, I thought, the tired smell of people stuck in one place for too long, of no sleep and little pay. I turned to go down to my bunk, then stopped, irresolute, and turned up to the wheelhouse.

"Hey," the skipper said.

He leaned over the console, looking at the gauges, and I saw the .44 behind him on the sill. I think he meant me to see it. I stared at it and felt the silence moving. But I climbed into his chair and took the wheel when he asked me to.

"The guys are tired," he said. "I'll let you go for a good long time."

I nodded. He watched me for a while, then shut the door and walked away.

I sat to steer, feeling the rhythm of it returning and the old fear of running someone else's boat, being perpetually half in the wrong in all the myriad small decisions. "Don't think," skippers say, "just do." But every moment you have to be thinking. You have to be alert and judging little things. So you're thinking and not thinking, you're subservient in a shit job with no way out, ever responsive to someone else's moods in little ways, feeling the irritation of being too long, too close together and never having enough time to sleep.

Hours slid by. I heard Mike breathing too close to me, a phlegmy, gasping, broken sound when he shifted or looked up out of his bunk to glare at the back of my head. I was still steering, long past midnight, when he got up and stood behind me. He breathed harder, as if to frighten me.

After a while he said, "If you sink this boat, you'd better drown. Because I will find you in the water and kill you."

I didn't answer. I felt myself get angry. He snorted and went back to sleep.

Late that night, with him in the room, I left the wheel with the autopilot on. I went down to the galley for a snack and saw the guys huddled at the table. They were whispering to each other, but when they saw me come in through the door, they fell silent and stared at me.

In a moment, the conversation began again, barely loud enough that I could hear.

"Least it's a job."

"He's not crazy; he's just a cocksucker. . . ."

"One of these days, he'll find out what I'm made of." Their words had a strange, repetitive air, like the wind itself or the waves wearing on the same spot in the mind, an endless, dizzying, wearying motion, questioning now if I'd join in.

"You can push a guy so far, and then . . ." Bill's eyes still watched me.

"He'll find out. Can't have it all his way."

I nodded and chucked some popcorn in the microwave. Stood with my back to them, waiting for it to pop. The tray went round and round behind the door. The light shone yellow, and the timer counted down. The smell of fake butter filled the room. I watched the kernels jump inside the bag and the bag puff up. When the paper started to brown, I took it out.

"Hey," I said again when I walked past. I knew this kind of boat. This dense feeling part fear, part anger; these men corroded with the cumulative weight of too many minor humiliations, in a situation they felt they couldn't leave.

"Hey," they said, after a beat.

Up in the wheelhouse, I slid back in my seat. It was getting shittier out. There was no shelter, only the bare islands of the Shumagins. I had the red light on while I steered, so I could see the instruments and see out. It looked warm, but it was cold. Snow built up on the glass and slid away. I counted down the minutes until the end of my watch.

An hour and forty-three.

An hour and forty-two. I wished I had a radio to play—something, anything, to keep me awake, so I wasn't so alone. But there was just the GPS with its coded numbers:

SOG: 7.5 knots

ETA: Never

The autopilot hissed back and forth. I kept my eyes on the screen. Outside, all I could see was dark water, the rain, and the blackness of the ocean. The shock of spray as swells struck the bow. Once I began to nod and woke up scared as a gull shot past us up the window, bright as a rocket in the sudden glare of light.

At 3:00 a.m. the wheelhouse door opened. It was Mike. He stood there again, watching. Reached down and changed the course slightly.

"Should ride a little easier now," he said. "Next time we're getting thrown around like this, wake me up."

I nodded. But I'd already sucked it in, the palpable tension on the boat.

He went downstairs and came up with the older guy.

"Bill's gonna take over. You can hit the rack."

I got up. Bill slid into the seat, warm from me sitting there. I went downstairs and crawled into my bunk. It was so loud I thought I wouldn't sleep. But I dropped off as soon as I lay down, feeling sick and groggy and very tired.

We reached King Cove early in the morning and tied up at the company pier. The cannery crew ran the pump into our hold, flooded it fresh, and drained it with the cod. We sat waiting inside the door, listening to the pump and the mixed rain and snow falling on deck. The cannery buildings and bunkhouses squatted on bare rock. No one wanted to go ashore.

When the pump had sucked out all that it could get, Mike sent us down into the hold to pitch the rest. They were ugly fish, gray and soft with age. The foreman complained to Mike, saying he'd kept them in the hold too long.

"Brought 'em straight here," Mike said. "Kept 'em circulating all the way." He stood over the foreman until he backed down.

"All right, all right." But the foreman crossed the dock and yelled down at us in the hold, "We ain't got all day."

Another worker tossed us each a Coke. I grabbed mine, not wanting to want it so.

Back inside, the kid stripped off his rain gear, leaving it slumped and empty by the door. He sat down and picked up his iPad.

"You got a sister?" Mike asked me.

"No," I said.

"Bill here would like to meet your sister."

I looked at him. He seemed almost catatonic, blue light on his face and his mouth gone slack.

But he glanced up. "My sister killed herself last spring," he said.

"I didn't say a fucking thing," I said.

And Bill, the older guy, said while peeling off his boots, "No date for the prom."

They both began to laugh. I looked back up the stairs and saw Mike's face. He was watching from the galley steps. I heard him go upstairs and close the door.

That night I dreamed about Iraq again. What it felt like to be there, the sense of waiting. There was a blind and legless man who used to sit begging on the stairs, at the corner where the bus no longer came. His hands were covered with calluses like feet. When you gave him coins, he spat at you. But we gave to him anyway, more than to the others. There was something about his radical misery that attracted us. It made us feel better somehow, in a way you didn't want to think about.

Half-awake, that dream blended with another, another boat, the first one I worked on when I was young, long before I went into the military. The skipper was blind but he pretended he could see. We used to wait on deck for hours for him to find the gear. No one would say anything at all. Then I thought about Iraq again, and how one afternoon we filled a canteen with sand and gave it to the man on the stairs. But even that had been nothing like this.

At 4:00 a.m., we reached the first string of gear. It was a short one, just a few pots they'd dropped to test near False Pass. The skipper called down, we kicked our gear on and went out. The wind shrieked across the water like it wanted to blow us off, and the deck was coated with a fresh inch of wet, slippery snow. Bill leaned over the side, peering forward through the dark, a buoy hook clenched in his right hand. When he saw the buoy, he yelled and lunged to catch the line. It caught with a wrench that knocked him off balance and smashed his face into the rail. He lost his grip and the buoy skated away, rising up the face of a breaking sea.

"Jesus Fucking Christ," Mike swore over the loud-hailer so angrily we jumped. "Get it together. I didn't hire a bunch of girls."

The kid turned on me. "Cut bait," he said.

Blood smeared Bill's nose. He rubbed it with a wet, gloved hand.

I grabbed a brick of frozen hake and hacked at it. A head split off and danced across the deck. Inside, the fish was marbled pink and blue in patterns like an anatomical dummy. Mike shouted again inarticulately, and Bill lunged forward to hook the buoy. This time he got the line through the block. He brought it in, letting the buoy trail back until the pot mashed against the side.

"About fucking time, Jesus Fucking Christ . . ." Mike's voice grew thin over the hailer, as if he was running out of air, but he kept swearing as monotonously as the wind. I ducked my head under a palpable rain of rage, corrosive, frightening, humiliating.

Bill and the kid dragged up the pot and heaved it over onto the launcher. The kid leaned inside and undid the trap. A mass of cod spilled thrashing to the deck, wide mouths gaping for water.

"Lousy catch," Bill said. "Fucking lousy."

He looked up and saw me.

"Don't just stand there," he snapped. "Get us the bait." Shit flows downhill.

I hustled forward with the filled container, slipping through the pile of fish. Bill kicked them aside. I crawled into the pot to clip the bait container to the rim. Perilously it rocked on its launcher. For a moment, I felt the vertigo of the deep. I scrambled backward, desperate to get out.

The other two leaned their weight against it. The pot struck the water heavily, paused and sank. The ocean closed over and it was gone, leaving only blowing snow and the dark water welling under the rail.

"Bag's on the rail," Mike shouted.

Bill grabbed his hook and lunged for the next pot, while the kid kicked fish toward the hold.

"We're gonna stack these out," Mike said. "Move west."

The guys looked at each other. My heart sank.

This time, when we hauled the pot we did not launch it. The other two pushed the coil of line into it and dragged it back. Their feet skidded on ice. They worked with angry force.

"The fucker does this every time," Bill said. "Can't fucking find a fish to save his life."

*You had a nice load last time,* I thought.

As if he read my mind, he said, "Those other fish? Those weren't ours."

I didn't ask. It could have been nothing or anything. I didn't care. I felt the familiar ache of work returning and I thought, *How could I have missed this so much?* But before, there'd been the promise of war. And in the war, there'd been the promise of home. And now I was home, in my own country, what promise was there? I worked angrily, too, against who knew what; some authority must have put me here; it wasn't me; it couldn't have been. It wasn't life. Life was elsewhere, elsewhere, someplace warm.

I slipped and fell. Got up and tried again. Again I fell, off balance. I worked badly, thrown by rage, my body no longer tuned to the boat. I felt others drawing away from me. We were not a crew; we were only here at the same time. For long moments, I couldn't even remember their names. So there was no relief, no relief at all. Because we couldn't pull together.

It took two hours to haul and stack the string. By then the sky began to pale with dawn. We went back into the galley to wait. It felt colder than it had been; I was so tired. Tired from the sea, a sore spirit, and loneliness.

"How far to the next?" I asked.

"Couple three hours. We got most of our gear farther west." Bill pulled off his boots, looked at his feet. "I got some kind of fungus going on."

The kid looked up. "You looked pretty fucking funny getting out of that first pot. Thought you were gonna shit your pants."

"There ought to be a fucking safety," I said.

He spat and shrugged, holding my eye. Something seemed to move deep in his gaze, like the look of water when the pot went down.

I flushed and looked away. I couldn't think of anything to say.

He went on, "You know Bill's done that, right? Guy he didn't like, just launch the pot a little early. Cut the line. Who'd ever know? Who'd know? It could've been an accident, so easy."

"Good bait," Bill said.

I laughed uneasily, but neither of them joined in. The kid sat shuffling the deck of cards. Bill stood up and put bacon on.

"Least you don't get sick," he said at last. "Nothing worse than pukers. How many eggs?"

"Four for me," the kid said. "Mike takes four, too."

"Fuck Mike," Bill said. But he broke twelve in the pan, and scrambled them in oil with his fork. When the food was ready, he slapped it on four plates and handed one to me with a spoon.

"Take that to the wheelhouse," he said.

I took it up, unlatched the door, and went inside. Mike was steering, hunched over the wheel. The room looked blue with smoke.

He stubbed out his cigarette. "Thanks," he said, and reached for the plate. He gestured out the window with his chin.

"Another hour," he said. "I'll steer. You better get some sleep." His face looked exhausted; his lips folded shut in a line.

"Yes, sir," I said. I hesitated, then went downstairs. Bill sat rubbing a long, blue bruise across his face. He flushed when he saw me, looked away.

An hour later, Mike called us up again. We hauled gear until late afternoon, but our catch was bad. At four we started picking up gear again. We stacked out thirty pots on deck and headed west, out through False Pass as it grew light. An hour later, we started laying gear. After we'd set it, we turned around, picked up the pots we'd launched, and stacked them again.

That day we worked until long after dark. By midnight, the weather had picked up so much, we couldn't handle it. Fifteen-footers, a sharp, steep swell with no more than a beat between each crest, and the wind chop tearing sideways across the top. Spume swept along the deck, glazing it with ice, and soft ice built up in the rigging. Mike called us in and pointed the boat around. I thought he meant to ride with it, but he headed east. He must have planned to run for shelter.

We kicked off our gear at the galley door. My fingers were so cold, I couldn't bend them. Bill grabbed a half-empty sack of cookies and shoved a handful into his mouth. I pushed past him and headed for the wheelhouse. The door opened. Mike looked out.

"The forecast's shitty," he said. "Pack ice moving down from the north." His face worked, and his eyes were bloodshot.

"Fucking wreck my pots," he said. "Fucking lose them. I said lost gear comes off the top, all right. Right?"

None of us answered. I nodded, though I knew he hadn't. He went back inside the wheelhouse and shut the door. I heard him thump the console with his fist.

"Fuck!"

The guys looked at me again. I thought they'd speak. The room filled up with what they didn't say. And I sat there, staring at my empty plate. Until the moment passed. Bill stood up. He slipped in a movie, something with guns.

"You should like this," he said. "See your buddies in it."

I hadn't told them where I'd been, but they knew. It was pretty hard to hide sometimes.

"Yeah, maybe," I said. I stood up, scraped my plate into the garbage.

Mike came back out of the wheelhouse again. "Bill, I'm gonna want you to get back out there and fix those pots with the broken pucker straps. You might have to bend the door on that one, too. Get 'em so's they're not leaking anymore."

"Now?" Bill began to say, softly, almost incredulously.

"Now? Fuck yeah, I mean now. We're gonna move back where we were. I think we were in 'em; we just got robbed."

Bill stood up very slowly. Mike closed the door back to the wheelhouse. "You, Hank," he said to me over his shoulder, "you got an hour down."

It was my turn to sleep. But I watched for a moment, too tired to go. Bill moved across the room with a kind of paralytic grace and opened the cabinet below the sink. He pulled out alcohol in a plastic bottle. Took a long drink and handed it to the kid. The kid swallowed. Handed it back.

"Now, I'm gonna put on my rain gear," Bill said. "Cheap Chinese, that fucking shit that's leaked since Dutch. I'm gonna go back out on that goddamned deck because that cocksucker can't catch a goddamned fish. I'm gonna go. I'm gonna do it for him. Because why? Because I'm a fucking pussy. That's why. Because I ain't had time to kill him yet. Because he ain't the worst fucker in the harbor, and it beats fucking pumping gas." He took another drink. "That's just exactly what I'm gonna do.

"You can push a guy just exactly so far, and then he's gotta show what he's made of."

I went down into the fo'c'sle, turning the handle so it didn't even click.

It was hot there from the engine. The air felt close and thick. Someone had tacked a child's drawing to the ceiling a long time ago. The paper was dusty and split along the thumbtacks that held it to the wall, and the colors had begun to run together. Thick chalk lines of a green tree. An orange sun. And two people standing side by side, one small with yellow hair in pigtails under a sky of impossible, perfect blue. I wondered whose kid it had been, where they were now.

Then I looked at water stains on the ceiling. The blurry shapes.

I had a friend in camp who shot himself. Afterward, people said he'd been in too many situations. They had a name for it. PTSD. But I always knew that it was just the wind, how it kept blowing. How he hadn't gotten mail that day, and it was his day to clean latrines. It was just the wind, no special reason why it happened that day and not some other one. It was hot there, and the sun just hung above us. You couldn't get away from it. You couldn't get away.

But after a while you have to change the game, to fight back in whatever way you can. I knew why he did it. It doesn't help.

Looking at the wall, I felt already dead and buried. In a steel cave, on the boat where life was to have begun again, but the shine was gone, and in its place there were no new dreams, only the intolerable weight of waking.

I flicked out the light and lay trying not to think. Water drummed against the hold and ice thumped and creaked along the waterline. We jerked against it, laid over by the wind. I felt a cold seep of fear start down in my chest. It built until I was almost panicking. Each time the sea thudded against the side it sounded as if it would break clear through. I breathed hard, fighting for control.

I got up then. I found a chisel and hammer in the tools and went into the engine room to squat on the floor, banging on steel almost mindlessly. I couldn't have said what I meant to do. But when the steel rebounded I lay down, staring at the picture and the shapes of yellow water stains on paint that had once been white.

I must have slept, because I woke at 4:00 a.m. to a sound I knew. I woke, already knowing something was wrong, on my feet before I knew I was awake.

"It's happening," I thought, not knowing what it was, only that I'd been expecting it for a long time. The boat had stopped, the engine still running, and as I stared the lights went dead.

I slid down out of my bunk and ran upstairs through the galley. Someone had fastened the wheelhouse door. I felt it press back when I hit it. Through it I heard the shouting. Inarticulate. Violent. And something slammed against the door. Someone wept.

"They're killing me. You're killing me."

A high, thin scream like a child's.

I threw my shoulder against the door. The catch broke. Inside, bodies thrashed back and forth in the dark. I saw the gleam of metal, catching the glow of dying instruments. I waited for a shot that didn't come.

"Help me," someone said. "Help me."

I dropped to my knees and felt a body, warm, resistless on the floor. I lurched across it and tackled someone around the knees. He went down, crashing against the wall. I flung myself across him and gouged at his face, striking the soft, rubbery flesh until the feel of it grew wet and he went limp. Behind me, the other man began to stir. He scrabbled to his knees, reached out, and grabbed someone behind me.

When the lights came on I saw Bill lying where I'd knocked him. The skipper hung on to the kid's throat. Blood poured down his hairy chest from a series of three light gashes in his throat. In one of them I could see his trachea work, a whitish slippery slimy thing, and there were punctures in his chest from which another bloom of blood seeped out.

He let go of the kid when he saw me. The kid slumped to the floor.

"Get lines," Mike said. I ran downstairs, hit the galley lights and glanced around. I was so dizzy I could hardly think, a feeling I knew and hated. But I saw no lines. I grabbed two rolls of duct tape and ran upstairs.

"Good enough," Mike said. He grabbed Bill's hair, yanked him upright and lashed the tape around his hands tightly enough to break the skin. Rolled him over. Threw a second wrap around his mouth.

Bill groaned. His eyes came open.

"He's going to fucking choke," I said.

"I wish he would," Mike said. He threw another wrap of tape

around Bill's legs, then turned to the kid. The kid screamed when Mike grabbed him. His arm hung at a bad angle from the socket.

"Easy," I said. But Mike kept on. He lashed them both together to the skipper's chair. Their eyes went wide, showing the whites and veins. Bill was bleeding from his nose. It bubbled up each time he gasped.

Mike handed me the tape. "Wrap my cuts, but not too tight," he said.

As I did, I met the kid's stare. He looked betrayed. And suddenly I wondered what I'd done. Whose side I'd chosen, and why.

"Those pieces of shit," Mike said thickly, seeing my gaze. The bandage on his throat swelled and contracted.

He looked at the others, drew back his foot, and kicked Bill hard. Bill groaned. Mike kicked him again and then the kid, systematically. His face wrenched so that I did not know whether he hated them or himself, and the boat kept swinging, banging in the swell, an endless, maddening, wearying motion.

Unaccountably, I remembered a man beating on a dog on a leash on the street in Iraq. I was on sentry and had nothing to do but watch. The street was heavy and empty and hot, full of a reality as brittle as glass. The man stood in the middle of it, knobby-bodied, dark. He hauled slowly forward on the dog, struck it, then let it go and hauled it forward again. The dog whimpered in an agony of fear. Whimpered, trying to roll over. I wanted him to bite the man, and he did not. They only moved together and apart as if dancing, held in a bond that went far past the leash.

The man looked up and saw me watching him. As if I had broken the rules of the game, he spat. He was not from there. A dark man, maybe Indian, I thought. I had no way of knowing. I was just a kid. When his eyes left the dog and looked at me, the dog rushed forward and tried to bite him. He kicked it hard in the groin, stared at me again, his eyes fathomless, as if I had something he wanted—youth? A ticket out?—and dragged it off down the rubble-strewn street, baking under the winter sun.

The door clashed shut, and clashed again, banging on the hook that'd held it often before, before we had slipped across so easily from what was done into what was imagined all too often. And suddenly, I knew what they'd been thinking. I felt the seduction of murder, how it seemed that it could change the game. And a wave of weariness washed over me. I felt so sad it was like I couldn't move. Because I knew then it was all a lie. They wouldn't ever kill the skipper. I couldn't leave the past. We would keep on like this day after day, and some days would be good, some days not. We'd think about these things like we could change them. But it would be the same now and forever.

≈ ≈ ≈

That night, we made it back to False Pass and tied up to the company pier. No one was at the cannery, but Mike called the Coast Guard on our sideband. They sent a chopper out to pick him up. It came in loud and landed on the pier. They got Mike on a stretcher and the others cuffed.

The chopper lifted and turned back to Dutch Harbor. But they left me there a little longer, to watch the boat in the absence of anyone else. I stood there waiting, watching them go. And I wondered if what I had done was right. What if it wasn't up to me to choose? I stood on the deserted pier, looking out and wondering. Looking at the sea drift floating by. A foam-flecked gray feather. A bit of trash.

But I knew then I would never change. None of us would. It was like war, this violence that stirred up before the world fell back on its old course. We all wanted to be on top of the heap, but it wasn't any better being there. So I waited for the chopper to take me on.

That winter the two of them went to jail. And the rest of us went back out on the water. After a time I drifted on to Thompsen's Bay. And Mike did, too, and the others, later. And all of us came not to be friends, but to acknowledge each other on the dock. Tacitly, we agreed to get along. We saw each other sometimes around town, from one boat to another, from year to year. It was a crime, but how it folds into a life.

# EASTER, THOMPSEN'S BAY

It was warm that day, the first real day of spring. The air smelled of the bitterness of alders and of soil released from the snow. Down by the lake, still bluish white with rotting ice, a group of kids threw stones out over the surface, scuffling a little in that strange, almost ritual way they had of interacting, the nascent spring rising in them, too.

A girl inched out across the ice, skinny legs too pale to be so bare, her hand still holding onto a boy. She dropped his hand and skated farther out toward some dark object on the ice, a knapsack, tossed there in the scuffle. Her friends watched, laughing at first, then quieted.

"Hey," I called, but suddenly everything moved too slowly.

Delicate and tentative as a deer, the girl slid outward. She grasped the bag, whirled to hold it up, and in that quick motion seemed to fall. Farther down the shore, a man turned at her sharp cry and the lake-ice crack. I saw the small, dark body of the girl vanish from one second to the next in the outlet above the river.

He reached the shore before I did, pushing through the children, throwing down his bike. Running to the hole in the ice.

"Grab a pole, anything," he shouted to me.

But there was nothing to grab. I glanced around futilely, caught one boy's arm.

"Call 911," I thrust my phone at him. He did; others were already dialing. Thank heaven then we are all so connected. I kicked off my shoes and plunged in after the man, through shards of ice stained with turbid water. I'd been a strong swimmer once, but now my body resisted me, too slow for this.

He surfaced, water streaming down his face, sucked air, and disappeared. I followed, peering through the amniotic lake looking for the girl, for the shape of disaster not yet quite accomplished.

The next time he rose, I grabbed his arm and dragged him down to what I'd seen.

When he rose again, he was carrying the girl, a limp mass, her hair a river down his back. He dragged her to shore, spread her out on earth still filmed with ice, and worked over her unresisting body until the long wail of the ambulance, its blue flashing lights, left us suddenly irrelevant.

Cars clustered in. People called out. They knew one another. I saw the face of the girl's mother. It wasn't one I recognized. Though I'd known her, too, I realized later. I'd known the girl, seen her around. But I'd never really looked at her until that moment, when I saw her finally, caught under the ice, her mute blue face blossoming in the dark. Her numb lips, her hands. Her white, frail neck.

≈ ≈ ≈

Later, driving home from the debriefing, I caught myself going too fast, thinking of the girl. The face of the mother I never really met. A cop car flashed its lights at me. And instead of stopping, I accelerated, thinking, "Is this really me? This can't be me." The needle rose past ninety, hovered there. I drove as if released from something. Behind me the siren began its long wail, until, responding to an instinct as abrupt as the one that set me in motion, I saw a pull-out and backed out of sight. I cut the lights in time to see the cop flash past.

For a long time, I sat listening to the tick-tock of cooling metal.

Hearing the truck settle slightly, branches shift, and night rise back in. Shaking with a delayed fear, mind blurred with release, the terrifying lucidity of action gone. My chest felt constricted, as if I couldn't breathe. I thought of that other body so abruptly stilled.

After a while, I picked up my cell phone. Scanned through the list of contacts. Clicked it shut.

When I reached home, Call met me at the door. I looked past him, my eyes adjusting from the dark.

He stepped forward, his shadow bisecting the light.

"I was about to call the cops," he said. "I was worried about you."

I sat down to pull off my shoes, unable yet, unwilling to talk. The words seemed too heavy. It would take too long and he might not understand. If I could lean on him, I thought, it might be different. But he never liked to just hold me.

"She was beautiful," I wanted to say. Again that numb face blossomed in my mind, the eyes blue as petals, half opening on the gurney but not with life.

His eyes pricked with concern. He sat down. Not near enough. Reached out to cup my shoulder as if weighing fruit, a mild, familiar coolness in his touch.

"It's not your fault," he said.

I nodded for his sake, but my body stiffened. That wasn't the point.

≈ ≈ ≈

Sunday, Call went to the harbor before breakfast. I went out but soon turned back to the over-silent house. I felt dislocated, jarred outside my life. The objects in the room stood mute, detached, the purpose that had connected them fallen slack. A cup dried in the rack; a fly buzzed on the sill near an unwashed plate from a meal eaten alone. Other than that, the air was still. Contained. It was a house where too much time had been spent unused, like the setting for a play that had been called off.

I moved across the room, pulling a curtain straight, picking up the plate.

A message blinked on the answering machine.

I poured another cup of coffee before I pushed the button, glancing at the machine. Waiting. As if, as long as I hadn't listened to it, it could still be something to hope for. A step into the future. Something to do. Or as if I knew already who it would be.

"Alice. This is John calling. The man from the lake. If you remember me . . ."

I finished the cup before I dialed the number.

≈ ≈ ≈

When I reached the lake that afternoon, John was waiting, watching ducks dabble along the bank. First of the season. His pants had ridden up his ankles. It made him look slightly helpless, his ankles too nakedly exposed, white and bony above his socks.

He looked up when he heard my footsteps. Happiness flashed in his eyes, as if he hadn't expected me to come.

"Would you like to feed the ducks?" he said, holding out a bag of bread. "They say it's bad for them, but they enjoy it."

I took a handful of stale crumbs and sprinkled it along the bank. The ducks flocked in, gabbling in pleasure. Watching them, I, too, wanted to laugh. When I took another handful, his fingers brushed against my wrist.

"How've you been?" he said. "I've seen you out walking."

"All right," I said. I moved a step away. "Where do you live?" I asked, surprised to realize I didn't know. Then my posture softened. I opened my hand and released the bread.

"For me, for me, that's nice, that's nice," the ducks seemed to say. I dusted the flour from my palms and smiled at them ruefully. They examined me for more, craning their necks to view me from small, wise eyes. The drake plopped busily into the water. The hens followed, scuttling to catch up. The bands on their wings caught the light, an iridescent, watery blue. It was the brightest color in sight. I'd worn drab all week, since the morning I'd pulled on a pink sweater, and startled by myself, looking down at my body, I pulled it off. I hadn't thought of myself as in mourning—I didn't know how—but still the color seemed obscene.

He'd been speaking.

"I'm sorry," I said. "The ducks . . ." He smiled. It didn't matter.

"That big house above the lake," he said. "Near the turn-off to the highway. I paint out on the porch in the morning, so I see you walk past. I like to see you."

I sat down before I answered, the distance between us carefully calibrated. Smoothed my skirt over bony, abrupt knees.

"What do you paint?" I said, though I knew.

"Birds," he said, certain of himself on this ground at least. "But maybe not birds you'd recognize. Sometimes I'll paint a single bone for months." He tried to explain how the articulated bones of the bird, smooth angles shaped by necessity, showed him what was more than the living bird.

"You can't just paint a robin," he said. "You have to paint past sentiment somehow. Sometimes, my birds don't look like forms. Instead, I see the blocks of colors. Or the lines between one part and another. Sometimes I organize things with my eyes, find a balance between you, the bench, the lake. Or in the birds, find the underlying structures."

I looked at the lake. The surface was silver now, all the ice gone. Where it had been, the water poured smoothly down into a tongue that entered the river before breaking into small, sharp, standing ridges where the flume narrowed in, constricting it. Over and over, the ripples curled and broke.

"Can you paint the girl?" I said. For a moment, I couldn't remember her name. "Jessie."

"I've tried," he said. His eyes followed mine. A woman walked along the dam. "It comes out wrong."

I shifted, chilled, the bench growing hard under my buttocks, but I didn't move on. A palpable awareness rose between us. I leaned against it, feeling its ebb and flow as I talked, gesticulating, or as he shifted his weight.

Late afternoon, he touched me first. Our faces leaned together, mouths fastened, lips closing on each other, tongues opening the inner reaches. Our teeth collided softly, moved apart.

His hand rode up my thigh, felt the concavities of my spine. I latched my fingers around his neck, feeling the pulse break lightly under them, the tenderness. The pressure of touch smoothed out some barrier between flesh and flesh, so that I felt my fingers feeling him, and how it felt to be him, to be me. In my mind, I saw us from a distance, two strangers leaning into an embrace. My gray wool coat, his jacket, the cold lake. Then the distance between us collapsed again, the surface of my mind wholly given over to the kiss.

"Come with me," he said softly in my ear. He led me from the bench into the trees.

Out of sight, he stopped in a clearing full of dry leaves. He spread his jacket on the ground for me to lie on, a courtly gesture. Let his cold hands slide over my breasts, undoing my clothes with unexpected facility. The wind broke over my bared flesh. Suddenly, I felt almost panicky, as clumsy as a teenager, as ardent and as innocent.

He mounted me, thrusting unevenly, his old man legs exposed to the sky. My arms wrapped so tightly around him, our breastbones ground together when he came. My head pressed almost painfully into his throat.

Afterward, he rolled back in the leaves. I did the same, looking upward where two hawks swam high overhead, disappearing into blue. Not covering myself, though he could see the scar from my appendectomy, the light folds of my abdomen where the skin was beginning to sag. My jutting ribs.

He took my hand and held it. My head nudged against him. We lay together quietly.

≈ ≈ ≈

Next time we met, we smoked a joint. Sun fell through the trees chill and bright. I could smell last year's leaves under our backs, sweat, the smokeless burn of decaying earth. Blue distances beyond the budding trees and the sharp green-gold of new leaves. It all seemed filled with wordless significance. I remembered things I hadn't thought of in years.

He ran his fingers through my hair, letting the strands fall back over the bone.

"I haven't done this since I was a kid," I said.

"I think it's been in my freezer for a couple years," he said. "I guess I knew I was saving it for something." His face relaxed. It looked more open, younger than it had been.

"I quit when I got married," I said. "I can't think why. I guess it was just that Call didn't smoke." I took a long drag, held it. Exhaled, and passed the soft, moist stub. It came partly unrolled between my fingers. "I'm getting old," I said. "I can't control these."

He breathed in smoke too deeply, laughed and choked. I laughed, too, though the joke didn't deserve so much. It was as if our laughter had been stored up like the weed, waiting for use too long past the pull-by date, until its savor was nearly gone.

≈ ≈ ≈

We met three more times that summer, always outdoors, always in the park. There wasn't much to talk about. Only this painful need, this shared isolation. To him, at least, I didn't have to explain. And the fire in him seemed as obvious and inevitable as the crocus curled up in the earth.

Afterward I closed my eyes, looking at the sky. The day left photographic tracers across my vision, negative images that renewed unexpectedly vivid each time I looked too quickly at the sun. It was a game I'd played when I was young, as if inflicting a light, avoidable pain somehow made the day more real. The brightness of it carried over, until life seemed charged with unexpected grace.

≈ ≈ ≈

By early summer, Call had drawn away from me. He didn't ask where I went when I left the house, but there was an absence in the air between us. At night, in sleep, he turned away from me. It reminded me of not long after we married, when for a season he'd fallen for a girl who worked on the dock. Then, too, he'd had that same sense of harshness, of futility. He grew angry easily with little things.

"Fuck this," he said, over and over. The girl was someone I knew. She wore her hair in long, black braids that fell over her shoulders, framing a face that was nearly pretty, vivid anyhow; and when her hair slipped back, she pulled it forward. She knew it was her best feature. I wondered if it was that hair that Call loved best, if it could make a tent that told a man he was alone and cherished for a time.

I liked her, though, strangely enough, despite the little air of meanness that had already begun to cramp her lips. I thought she neither liked nor disliked me or Call. But when she was near, his body language grew more eager, exaggerated. He preened himself half unconsciously. I'd see them talking on the dock, their heads inclined toward each other. There'd be nothing in their conversation to alarm me, but I felt the closeness that surrounded them, as if I'd stepped inside a private room.

They turned toward me when I came near, but I knew they'd been happier alone. Whether they were aware of it or not, or could admit it even to each other, my presence was an intrusion.

It ended before I had to acknowledge it, or to be too wholly hurt by it. Before long, I saw her with someone else. Call was quiet for a while, then got drunk. But even after all these years, I remembered her. The memory formed a kind of otherness in me, a cleft in the roots of our marriage. Even in bed, sometimes I felt myself retreat. I never talked to Call about it, but I remembered it as a way out when our life together seemed too narrow. *He might even have been happier with her*, I thought, *with someone who would've been happier with him.*

≈ ≈ ≈

In August, I told John I could not come back. It was something I'd thought for some time, feeling the protective immediacy that had surrounded us begin to fade, as the crisis that pushed us together passed. But when the moment came, it seemed abrupt.

"John," I said. "I can't do this any longer." Either you leave your husband, or you don't.

He looked at me, stricken. I felt sick.

"I love you," he said. His words sounded unexpectedly fragile. I rubbed his chest, the shared sweat still drying from our bodies. His narrow chest, cooling, rose and fell. His breath came short. A kind of stiffness, a tremulous possibility, hung in the air.

"I love you, too," I said, but my words, too, were hollow. I didn't love him, not the way I loved Call, with the durable faith of many years together, of shared familiarities and disappointments. The love that can outlast even physical intimacy, for the sake of deep identity. John and I wouldn't grow old together; we'd never have that daily solidarity. We had nothing for each other but the present. I thought of Call during that summer with the girl and pitied him as I'd pitied myself.

John stared at the ground.

"So that's how it is," he said at last. He pulled on his clothes, covering his nakedness.

"That's how it is."

I looked away. My gaze felt like an intrusion. His hair, too, was fading. His fingernails were cut too bluntly, smudged with paint, visibly thickened with age and work. I was startled to see how old he looked.

He nodded, still not meeting my eyes. "Good-bye," he said, almost too easily. He walked away, his shirt swinging absurdly above his unfastened slacks. Some distance off, he stopped, his back to me, and did his belt, pulling it tight. He tucked in his shirt too carefully, as if it was the only thing he had left to do. There was no need to hurry ever again; there was no one waiting for him now.

He'd told me his house was much too large for one, submerging him so it must have seemed a long and weary trek out of his bed each morning, out of the isolation that buried him and his colors in the too-still room. Painting past sentiment, he said. Painting his grief. He walked off, as distant from me as he'd been before the morning of the accident.

≈ ≈ ≈

When I stepped through the door into the house, it struck me as strange it should be so unchanged.

# INNOCENCE

A line snapped up from the deck. Curled and disappeared. The other deckhand, horsing around. Paul had this idea he could learn to tie a bowline in midair. It was crazy irritating.

"That was weak, dude," Wyn called lazily. No answer.

Five hours still to Noyes Island.

Wyn's body stretched out, hot, uncomfortable, the aluminum grid of the skiff ridging his back. Light poured into the bowl of the lashed skiff and on the deck of the seiner below. The boat rocked to a steady chop that stung cold and salty along the side. Overhead, the boom creaked back and forth, moving a fraction of an inch each way before jerking tight against the rigging. A steel beam, familiar to him, so familiar he could feel its coldness, its blistered paint, against his palms without thinking of it or knowing he was doing it.

If he raised up in his seat the wind struck him, driving out the warmth. The sea was so bright it hurt his eyes; the islands too sharp a green and blue. Better to lie, drunk with light, his eyes closed against the sun, watching through the liquid curtain of his eyelids.

Thinking of Abby. He rolled over to conceal a sudden embarrassing hard-on, though there was no one in a position to see. If there was a girl on board . . . but there wasn't. Ed's daughters were too young.

If Abby was on board . . . he cramped up again with a gust of desire. Abby here, her small round butt bent over the sink. Abby's flat little boobs in rain gear. But Abby would never do that.

The line snapped up again, twitched against the sky and disappeared.

"Weak . . ."

"Shut up." Paul's grinning face lurched above the skiff wall and vanished, crapulous with red hair.

*Crapulous,* he thought. That was a good word.

Four and a half hours to Noyes Island. The deck cluttered with gear they were hauling north. The seine, line, a gas tank for tendering next season.

Overhead, he heard Ed's shout. His wheel watch. He dropped swiftly down onto the deck. Up in the wheelhouse, Ed stretched out, heels on the console, steering with one foot.

"Just keep her as she is," he said. Wyn slid into the seat. Ed stood up, adjusting himself, stretching, yawning, looking out over the stern.

"Nice day," he said. "Hope the weather holds."

Wyn nodded.

"You're gonna want to call me when we hit that island up ahead," he said. "I'll make the turn." He dropped down out of sight into the galley, easy in the plain authority of unquestioned intelligence. "We'll get in behind it; check on 'em before their pussies start hurting too bad."

His head disappeared. Wyn cued up the music. " . . . aa ah m," the vocal-less rhythm seemed to shake the dusty cigarette air of the wheelhouse. He pushed the window open. An albatross rode the air off their bow, the grayish kind. He felt a little sick now in the enclosed space. The boat jerked against the chop, jerked like a dog on a leash. Whoops. Crash. Whoops. Crash. Again and again.

On the radio, far off, he could hear two men talking, first about their sets. "Gotta thousand on that one." Longliners maybe. Then, "Gotta go make my baby. You should see the size of it . . . nothing worse'n a chili shit . . ."

Disgusted, he flicked the channel up, but the other channels just held static. He went back to the original; it scanned between eight, the chatter channel, and sixteen, for the Coast Guard. "Attention all mariners, attention all mariners . . . navigational hazard . . ." But it wasn't anything, only some logs reported drifting in Cross Sound. Hazard for the pukers. Not for them. Though sometimes drift from the logging barges choked up the tiderips heavy as popweed.

He sighed and shut the radio off. Four hours. He wondered how the others were doing down there. Where they were bound.

The sun rolled down the horizon overhead, touched the flat, blue line of open ocean, seemed to swell and bleed outward. Shadow swept across the surface of the water, hollowing the sea; then as the sun sank farther, the air seemed to thicken. The water held the light like a liquid substance, dense as mercury, glowing back up at the paling sky. No land now anywhere in sight. Even the mountains had disappeared in the hazy air of evening.

Wyn heard the galley door clang shut. Paul coming in, starting dinner. The smell of Easy Cheese and chili—they were sick of that. Burnt coffee. Popcorn. The four food groups.

Ed's snore, from the day bunk just below the hatch.

The fourth guy, Charles, had flown ahead.

Wyn settled back, tried to think again of Abby, but it was no good. Though she was always somewhere in his mind, lately when he tried to think of her directly he got depressed. It was something about the way she hung on him, and something about the men in the hold below, with their air of purpose larger than themselves. He lit a cigarette, though he knew he shouldn't, and blew the smoke slowly out the window. It met and mingled with a denser cloud, the exhaust blown forward from the stack, and the soot drifting from the oil stove. The wind had changed, setting against their stern.

He leaned forward. Looked out the back. Something seemed wrong.

≈ ≈ ≈

They'd picked the others up in Sunday Harbor, just north of the border. The night before Ed had told them what was up, reluctantly.

"Remember what we've done together," he said. Wyn got the sense that he liked none of this business, not the trip, not confiding in his crew. But he had no choice, if he was to do it. He couldn't get the men on board without their help.

"Just as far as Thompsen's Bay," he said. "And if anyone asks, we're heading back for repairs. Shit season, anyhow." And it was true; they could no longer keep fishing. When the gen-set blew three days ago, all three of them sat up in the wheelhouse talking until Ed chased the others out. The season wasn't worth the money to replace it, and Ed had let the insurance lapse, but without a chiller they couldn't keep on fishing. Already, they'd been shorthanded since July.

He didn't know how this new plan had come about. Someone had spoken to someone; someone else called. People knew that in the old days Ed had done time for moving grass up the coast from Washington, north, and had gotten busted off the Copper River when a load of brown shirts stopped him for questioning. But this seemed darker somehow, less of a game, and Ed himself didn't seem to know what they were playing on the edge of. He must have thought it over that night for a long time, before deciding to make the gamble. And thought it over further before the night he called them into his cabin for a conference.

"Are you in . . . ?" "We've got this opportunity . . ." "Run a load of Mexicans north, get the boat worked on. It'll pay us for our time." And maybe save our asses; he didn't say. But Wyn knew. Paul was still too young.

≈ ≈ ≈

They'd been told the others would be waiting by the crane on the disused dock near the Coast Guard station. Alone. And so they were. When they pulled in to the dock, Ed steering, Wyn in the bow of the skiff, five of them stepped quietly out of the shadows by the dock crane.

"Habla español?" one spoke in Spanish, inflected with some language Wyn didn't know. He shook his head. The man spoke again in English, halting, using the words they had agreed on.

Ed answered, "Maracaibo is a long way off."

Inexplicably, Wyn wanted to laugh, wanted to say, "Do people really talk like this? Is this for real?" But his heart was thudding.

"Get in," Ed said. One man stepped forward and slid over the gunwale into the skiff. He hadn't been in a boat before. He moved without the practical ease of a fisherman, stooping but not touching the gunwale, but he didn't seem afraid. It was as if this was only one small step in a journey that had begun so long before, there was nothing left for him to fear.

He said something in Spanish. The others followed, moving agilely over the rail. One of them met Wyn's eyes and smiled, a quick flash as quickly suppressed. A Saint Christopher medal hung at his throat, inside the open neck of his shirt. He saw Wyn looking at it.

"Catholic?" he said. He touched it.

Wyn shook his head. The man settled in the bilge, close against Wyn. So close in the crowded skiff that their shoulders pressed against each other. His skin felt cool with sweat under a cutoff, cotton shirt. So close Wyn could see the gaps between his teeth, already brown, could smell the rankness of days without fresh water, the closed-in fetor of other hiding places.

The other man smiled again, almost unconcerned, looking at the sea. Wyn would've liked to talk to him. He opened his mouth to speak.

"Hssh," another man said. The first one moved his head out of sight of the spotlight at the Coast Guard station. Its flash broke over the water, leaving the shadows, the late summer dark, darker still. The wind picked up lightly, fell away, coming from the open ocean. Wyn tipped his head back to look up at the sky and saw the other do the same.

When they reached the seiner, the men filed silently into the hold, each poised for a moment, on the brink, before dropping below.

"Wait," Ed whispered. He tied the boat off and climbed aboard, following their unlikely passengers.

Wyn got blankets for them from the fo'c'sle, taking one from each of the crew's bunks. Water. Earlier, when they back-stacked the seine, they'd gone down to make sure the hold was dry. It was small, maybe ten feet by fifteen, and too low for a man to stand up. It smelled of brine, of fiberglass and aluminum. The floor sloped into the central trough above the shaft alley, covered with a corroded grate. When they put the hatches on, it would be completely dark.

He sat down on his haunches for a moment, something he'd never done down there before, and tried to imagine what it would be like, in the pure dark during the crossing. What it would feel like to these strangers.

Down there, now, they settled with a soft sound, an animal breathing. Some words together, a muffled complaint. He'd wedged a bucket behind the stringers for what needs they might have, and he showed it to them now by flashlight, diffidently, not wanting to offend.

"That's the shitter. We'll stop when we can." Last thing, he handed them the flashlight, hoping they would know not to use up the batteries. Swung ably up out of the hold. It was a high jump even for him, and part of him wanted them to notice. He turned back and looked at the one with the medal, as if to tell him, "You're safe with me. I'll take care of you." Their eyes met.

When they laid the hatch cover back, he could hear them praying.

Once the men were stowed below, the crew hosed the deck and back-stacked the seine again, hand mucking it forward so that it partly covered the hatch, as if they'd stacked it sloppily, too tired. If the Coasties came aboard, it wouldn't be easy for them to check the hold.

Ed winched the skiff back up onto the deck.

"Make sure we're squared away for travel," he said and vanished onto the bridge, disinclined for talk. A distance had come over him. He knew more than they did, after all, about the cops; he seemed nervous, more frightened than the rest.

Wyn was still alight with adrenaline, but under that he, too, felt the deep undertow of weariness and of a doubt that was new to him.

Discouraging. He checked the lines, the boom was tight, nothing free on deck—and went up to the wheelhouse, too.

"I'll take the first watch," Ed said. "Get Paul up at two, and you can take over at four."

Wyn went below, but even sleeping, he could feel the alertness in the hold. What were they thinking? The bunk that had been so familiar grew oppressive. He felt the crumbs of foam bunching on the worn cover, the heavy, stale air. He thrashed under his blanket, not used to insomnia, not used to waking, knowing he was in charge of something, or to this delicate feeling of care, as if the others were an extension of himself, with their unknown purpose, the danger carried with them like an odor.

Upstairs, he heard the *scree-scree* of the chain-drive steering. Ed was still sitting there. Wyn wondered what Ed was thinking.

Past midnight he woke more fully, bathed in sweat. He got up. Up in the wheelhouse, Ed was steering still, though it should've been Paul by now. Wyn saw the slumped shoulders, the point of light that was a cigarette. Outside, a darkness lit by the deep, refracted glow of open ocean.

"Everything OK?" Ed said.

"Yeah," Wyn said, not sure why they whispered. "Want me to take over?" A ritual exchange from a season's worth of work.

"Yeah. I guess so." Ed stood up slowly. "I don't know what the fuck we're doing. Wyn?"

"Yeah."

"Nothing." He turned to go, looked out over the back. "You sure everything is squared away down there?"

"Yeah," he said.

He hesitated. In the silence, he heard it too, a steady tapping from the hold. Irregular, soft, someone communicating through steel.

"It stops if you go back there," Ed said.

"Might not be them."

He looked at Ed, and saw again the look in his eyes that'd been there when he came back from jail, something between decency and fear. Nudged open the door. Looked out on deck. Silence. The hiss of waves along the side, the wide, cold smell of far-from-land. The horizon only a lighter black. The water seemed to catch what light there was and cast it up again above the surface.

"Let's be on the safe side."

"Sure, boss," he said. "You want me to try to get back in there?" Inside, he hoped Ed would say no. He was suddenly afraid of what might have happened down there in the hold. What might be down there.

"Too hard while we're traveling," Ed said. "They'll be all right. After all, it's not too far." And it won't be enough, he didn't say, for any of us. "Wyn, they'll be fine. You gave 'em some chow, didn't you?"

"Yeah," Wyn said. "All right." He hesitated. "Guys like that . . . what's up with them?" he said.

"I don't know," Ed said. "And I don't want to know. They're just different. They're like . . . they have something to work for. You heard that, right? I don't know where they're going or why. But I almost kind of don't even want to charge them. Just take them on, as far as we can go. They can't have much.

"But you know. I think that, and then I think about my own bills. My own house. Guys like that—maybe it's just they can think of someone else. Something more." Ed looked around, at the wheelhouse. The candy wrappers. Styrofoam cups. Suddenly, he seemed very old, a wreck of a man, his body sagging heavily, unloved, unused.

"Yeah. Maybe," Wyn said, uncomfortably.

Ed turned to go. "Guess I need a snack," he said, then turned again and lay down on the day bunk without speaking. He crossed his arms over his chest. His breathing shifted, became lighter, not fully sleeping yet. A deeper stillness came into the room.

Wyn leaned back, looking at the radar. The compass bearing. No other visuals outside.

At four, Paul took over. Then Ed again. Wyn lay down, got up, made coffee, and went out to the skiff as the day warmed. The morning light made ripples across the deck, reflected pools of silver and gold. The sky turned opal to the east, a charmed light, as if they hung inside a limitless, perfect world. He lay watching it travel overhead. Now the men below seemed only men, the rapping gone, his fear gone, too. He was ashamed of his night thoughts. They were probably sleeping now, or trying to, their bodies cramped and constipated from a night at sea. And now their journey was only a problem to be solved, a set of tasks to get through until the day, tomorrow morning or late tonight, when they reached their destination and put the men off.

By afternoon, they were cheerful once again.

≈ ≈ ≈

Wyn eased his back as if he was an old man, pulled on his Mustang jacket, and stepped outside onto the deck behind the wheelhouse door. He flicked his cigarette over the side to extinguish it. It caught in the wake and tumbled under. More smoke drifted from the stack, a thicker mass, curling almost lazily, the cloud distorting, whipping away as the breeze caught it, puffing forth again.

He was thinking of Ed still talking in the dark.

"How did it get like this," Ed said. "That we're the ones so afraid of everyone else? Maybe it's cause we have too much, we're afraid of those who have less than us. But it's a goddamn shitty way to live. . . ."

Wyn held still, listening.

"We all die the same," Ed said. "Sooner or later, and for an awful lot of us it's sooner. Guess I'd rather have a reason when I go. Not have it be some stupid goddamn thing, a heart attack while I'm on the shitter at eighty, or dying so slow I can't remember who I am, all alone in a hospital bed pissing on myself. I guess these guys, at least they've got something worth dying for, back home. I guess I envy them that."

"Where do you think they're going?" Wyn asked again.

"God knows," Ed said. The silence deepened.

≈ ≈ ≈

The smoke whipped and curled out of the stack. Inside, the insulation began to smolder. A piece shriveled at the corners, blackened. It dropped onto the searing exhaust pipe. The thread of fiber burst into flame, and the flame ran upward, up the metal walls.

"We need to replace that before it fails," Ed had said, early in the season. But it hadn't seemed too urgent yet, not compared with all the other things to be done.

Now the epoxy bubbled at the rising heat. A larger piece fell against the pipe and flamed. At the base of the stack, the fiberboard inspection plate began to burn. The fan that cooled the engine room forced in fresh air.

Perhaps ten minutes passed between the first spark and the moment when the flames, already well established, broke through the stack and climbed the cabin wall.

Wyn stood looking out on the back deck at the smoke drifting from the stack. And suddenly, before the thought caught up to him, his feet were thudding down into the cabin. He was yelling, "Fire!"

The men jerked upward in their bunks. Ed ran outside and saw the first light tongues of flame spit forth, a liquid orange deepening to blue.

He grabbed the deck hose and spooled it up the wheelhouse ladder, slid the nozzle down into the pipe.

"Get the pump going," he yelled.

Wyn yanked open the engine room hatch, knocking back Paul who stood, mouth open, by the door. He wrenched the knob that turned on the hydraulics and hit the switch to start the hose. The water burbled up in a thin trickle, its pressure too weak to drive straight upward. The pump had always been a joke. The hose caught fire in the stack. The end melted. It fell truncated back to the deck. Paul grabbed it, squealing at the hot rubber, and tried to stretch it out again.

"Fire extinguishers," the skipper shouted. He heaved the big one out of the cabin.

Wyn caught it, and cranked it on. Paul ran inside to grab the other extinguisher from the bunks, then dropped it and dragged the survival suits out through the door now suddenly ablaze. Foam shot from the nozzle of the extinguisher, spraying the deck. Spraying Paul's knees. Coating the house that splintered into fire, the sound of it guttering in a roar. Wyn heard the windows snap. He closed his eyes and kept the foam trained on the flame.

The skipper scrambled to the bridge. He grabbed the mike. Wyn heard him call, "Mayday, Mayday. This is the fishing vessel *American Beauty.*" He gave their lat and long and dropped the mike. Grabbed the life raft, tearing it free from its restraints. Shouted to the deck, "Get your survival suits on, boys. We're getting off this thing. It's going to blow."

Paul grabbed a suit, and dropped it when Wyn shouted, hearing a sudden hammering underfoot. "The men," Wyn yelled.

Ed whitened and cried out, backing up as the fire blew higher, cutting him off from the deck.

Wyn grabbed Paul's arm. "Help me," he said. They seized the hatch. Below, the men were pounding at it. But the seine slipped over it, weighting it too much. Frantically, they tried to drag it back, a ton of mesh beginning now to smolder, fighting the web that piled and spread without a beginning or an end.

So it was they were still on board when the gas tank blew.

Wyn felt a mass of hot air lifting him, hurling him back, as if something had kicked him in the chest. It blew him out across the water. Stunned, he slammed against the surface, choking, deafened by the force of the blow. Behind him, the boat flowered into fire, rising in impossible liquid brightness into the astonished sky. The gas, exploding, doubled in the air. He saw the running flames of the seine as it dissolved into a molten mass, pooling down the side of the boat. The bluer flame that punched up from the diesel tanks and the percussive brightness from the laz. His ears cleared. And then the sound of yells.

Flame whistled out across the surface of the water. He thrashed backward. Behind him, the towering flame began to fall. Then the hull lay, a bowl of fire and smoke, flickering slowly lower, dense with light.

Far in the distance, he saw the skipper through searing eyes. He knelt in the life raft, miraculously afloat, a small, dark figure in the heat-shocked air. Nearer in, a single head bobbed unresponsive, too near the fire. He watched as it drifted closer to him, seeming now to swim weakly, erratically.

At last, when it came near, he saw it was Paul. His face was seared red, seamed with flame. One eye looked white. Periodically, he dipped his head into the surface. When Wyn grabbed his wrist, he started to chuckle.

"Are you all right?" Wyn yelled. He laughed harder. Flopped a little. Wyn gave it up. The boat was drifting away from them, a mass of light, still hissing as the flames sank down. The noise had stopped.

"It'll burn all night." Wyn's first lucid thought.

Far off, the skipper's arms were windmilling. He couldn't tell if he was waving or paddling. But even the light breeze seemed to bat him backward. He grew smaller, skating slowly off. The last they saw of him, he was alone, his arms still moving as he tried to steer the raft, like a water bug under the wide, blue sky.

Wyn felt an enormous weariness break over him. His arms seemed like lead, too weak to hold him up. But he tightened his grasp on Paul, who was mewling now, flapping his hands and still dipping his face beneath the surface of the water.

With some part of him detached, he wondered if anyone had heard Ed's Mayday. It seemed a question too distant and hard to answer. But he'd meant to do something. He'd needed to do something. What?

His mind drifted off. He shivered violently.

With a final effort, he tugged free the cord of his sweats and knotted Paul's wrist loosely to his own. But was that it? He felt oddly calm, only so tired.

Paul rolled forward.

Wyn thought he saw a crowd of people far away, all waving to him, going about some chore, a vast tide of bodies moving to and fro, starting and stopping, colorless with distance. But what were they doing? To what purpose?

Things fell away. He did not think of home at all, or even Abby. He felt as if he were trying to gather in thoughts that escaped too quickly from his net. Faster and faster they traveled, slipping away, and he himself was traveling with them, scattered and lost, into a point of light that kept receding even as he flew toward it. The giddy speed of his mind astonished him, traveling and traveling to the vanishing point, but the viewing eye did not lose sight of it, nor did it move.

He felt himself slide into distance.

When he woke again, Paul was dead. He moved his arm, and Paul's moved with it, unresisting. He floated facedown in the water. He'd been wearing nothing but a tank and sweats, and his back was burned a molten red. It hung under the surface, moving lightly in clear water, buoyant with baby fat. Wyn saw it, almost unmoved. He jerked his arm again, and watched Paul's follow. But he didn't try to cut the cord.

It occurred to him to wonder why he floated. He'd been the kind who could sink at will, a bony, lanky, graceless adolescent. He knew he must be wearing his Mustang coat, but he could not think when he had put it on.

The sun was lower now, but it hadn't set. The sky had turned a tremulous pale blue above the darker blue of open ocean. The moon was rising in the west, still no more than a smudge of light in the dim, whitening sky. He blinked at it. It seemed almost unbearably beautiful.

The water stirred. A strand of bull kelp traced past, smoothing their bodies.

The horizon stretched around them in a perfect circle, unbroken now even by smoke.

A seagull dipped down over his body.

"Damn you," he said. He jerked his head. In that motion, he seemed to break into life again. He choked on a cry, feeling his lips cracked, his eyes searing. A terrible thirst scourged into him, so that his tongue protruded from his aching mouth. His soul seemed torn out of his body.

"Help me," he yelled hoarsely. Hadn't anyone heard?

Wouldn't anyone come? The sky faded overhead. No lights in sight. He strained his ears for the sound of a plane. If they didn't come now, they never would. He knew he couldn't make it through 'til morning.

He felt himself dwindle to a speck on the wide blue plate of the Pacific. The ocean was so huge, so empty. He would sink so deep he wouldn't reach bottom, but drift suspended through the water, one of the bodies that were never found. Again his mind faltered. He began to sob. And then it seemed that someone was talking, words that babbled endlessly and would not stop. A dog barked far off, a ball bounced and fell, as if the people he once knew surrounded him and kept on passing.

He saw the men standing before him. One met his gaze, arms folded, floating absurdly above the sea, a blackened medal loose around his neck.

"What do you want?" Wyn dug his hand into his eyes. It seemed to him they weren't to be trusted.

"Pity," he said.

"I tried," he said. *Forgive me,* he thought. *I should have understood. Sometimes the hardest things go unrecorded.*

The wind flickered over the water, splashing a little salt against his lips.

Slowly, the pain seeped out of him again. The sun was gone now, leaving only sky. Again, he thought he heard something at last, but it was only wind and water whispering, not words. Somewhere he tried to hold on to the light. Somewhere, someone was asking him. If they would just stop. If he could just think. If he could listen long enough to hear . . . He would understand it all in time to . . . what?

His eyes swam open. It was so easy, finally. It was all right. He tried to say that. But there was no one left to tell.

The gull, returning, dipped low but did not stop.

# ANGEL HOTCH

The first time I saw Ed Hotch's daughter, she was standing on the riverbank below my house in a tangle of wild rosehips and raspberry vines, of fireweed stalks, birch bark, and dry grass. She'd pulled her skiff far up the silty bank, so that it lay pointing at the sky, and she stood there silently, her arms outstretched, holding out to me a pair of ducks. A Native girl, too young for me.

I looked at the birds, not knowing what to say.

"Your dad send these?" I asked.

She nodded, her eyes widening "Yes," holding out the birds in a gesture that seemed to both offer and forbid.

"Thanks," I said. I took them by their limp necks. Dried blood stiffened their pin feathers. She slid her boat back out into the river. Too late, I realized I should've helped and realized, too, she was older than I'd thought. I could never tell the ages of the girls of this place. They seemed unfamiliar, alien to me, more at home here than I could ever be.

"Good-bye," I said, or tried to. She yanked the throttle until the Evinrude caught. I watched until she faded out of sight against the dark line of the farther shore. The whine of her engine grew quieter, a thrum that seemed to take up all available silence, extinguishing it, until in the end the silence won again and settled back over the empty land. Then there was nothing but the water, wind, winter coming, and me standing before the cabin I'd wanted to build.

I turned and went back up the path again, where the last leaves were falling from the willows, rattling, dry with frost. Only a few remained, their color faded from its initial gold into dull brown. The river had fallen two feet from its high in June, last week's waterline marked with a scurf of yellow leaves. Where it had been the silt was hardening like stone, marred by my footsteps, the steps of caribou, and the ice crystals that broke the earth apart.

Already the sloughs had begun to freeze. The sky had grown white-blue with snow coming.

I thought there was no sky anywhere like the sky of this country.

≈ ≈ ≈

Next time I went in to town, I asked about her. They said her father was from back East. They said he'd killed another child, picked it up and swung it against the wall when it screamed too long one night. I didn't want to think that could be true. Everything here seemed larger than life. Besides, I thought, how could they have known what really happened in that family?

≈ ≈ ≈

The next time I saw her, it was January. I had the door wedged shut, chinked against the cold. The single window was blank with thick frost. It had been so long since anyone knocked; at the first faint scratch of sound, I looked around the cabin, thinking it must have been a vole. The Aladdin lamp wavered in a draft, almost fading out, and the dense ammoniac smell of unwashed flesh rose up around me as I moved. I was slipping then. It had been too long, the dark. I didn't know how to adapt to that place.

She knocked again. I went to the door, kicked the rags aside, and opened it. The cold crept in, in a cloud of steam that curled along the floor. At first I recognized her only by her height.

She'd come to stay, she said, but I wouldn't let her. She stood inside the door, her hair whitened with the frost, as I looked around the drafty, creaky, cold, and half-built room. Thinking she wasn't my problem. Not why I'd come north. And no one I wanted to be troubled by. Even knowing she might have nowhere else to go if not back home, even knowing that I could believe she'd be all right.

In the end, I made her go again. She walked off over the thick white slabs of windblast snow that covered the frozen river, leaving a track so marginal it meant almost nothing. But then, there was nothing else to remember in a landscape where everything was so swiftly erased. Just a few prints in places where the snow was soft enough to take a mark. A trail that might have been deeper, from my cabin to hers. And the blank snow that could cover anything.

≈ ≈ ≈

In February, she came back again. She carried a pack this time, which she set down outside the door. This time I brought her in. Offered her coffee. She closed the door behind her and tried to kiss me. Her face rasped on mine. Stepping back, she pulled off her parka. Her eyes never left me. But it was as if she wasn't really there, or was pretending she wasn't.

"Just come in," I said, at last. "Wait." But it'd been too long since I spoke. The words fell on the floor between us uselessly. She unbuttoned her shirt, pulled it off, and stood naked from the waist. Her small breasts trembled, not rounded yet. Her bones scooped out dark hollows of shadow. I thought if she would just stop looking at me, it might be all right.

Still, I hadn't seen a girl's body in so long. I felt a pressure in my groin. I moved closer, rubbed my hand along her neck where it bent out in abbreviated wing blades. She bent her head as if to accept.

Did she do that? Or was it only in my mind?

I realized I wasn't the first. I realized even then I shouldn't be doing this, though I guessed she was older than she looked. But I came quickly, and even though she had in a sense paid for the right,

I wouldn't let her stay. I was afraid someone would come for her. Maybe she was, too. But all the same, I couldn't forget what I'd done. How small she had still been. How indomitable.

≈ ≈ ≈

That May I heard she'd built herself a raft and escaped downriver after breakup. People saw her floating past the village, but no one tried to go out to her. The river was still thick with floating ice that piled and groaned in eddies and slow water. It shrieked almost like a person, booming and cracking in the warming air.

Then it was springtime and the ice was gone, leaving only scars, head-high, along the shore. The willows greened in a single night. Bluebells opened, then wild roses, and the bugs came out. That summer, I fished for dog salmon and sold them to the barge that came upriver. I built another shed, filled it with wood. Repaired the cabin that had been too small. I was learning, I thought, how to live here, in this wild place so far from anything I'd known. And the summer passed so quickly, even then. The long, light nights kept me working with a manic zeal to modify the land and make it mine—the land that still stretched, inexhaustible, out from the boundary of my cabin site in a long expanse of bluing hills, clouds, sloughs, and spongy muskeg, clear to Siberia without a road. It seemed it would never end; the land could not be hurt, nor Angel, nor me, either, not ever.

The days began to shorten again. I marked out traplines, welcoming the cold. It all seemed so fresh and new to me. I'd almost forgotten her, only something like an omen sometimes drifted across the face of summer days. When the sun still lay heavily on the land, and all day I didn't talk because there was no need to, or else stopped and set down my tools just to look at the young, unmarked country.

≈ ≈ ≈

Years passed before I saw her again. By then I was working, stringing pipe for the new Alaska pipeline. Money flowed like crude in those days. Every night we drank in the camps. I saw lines of coke stretched down the Fairbanks bars, fistfights erupting and settling away, sometimes in a crowd or sometimes in the long, strange light of ambulances, forgotten the next morning as the crews moved out, hungover, cursing, half awake. Some men came in from Texas, Alabama; others were homesteaders like me, tired of the isolation after all, of the wilderness that hadn't saved our souls, and the land that never offered all of itself. Hoping for quick cash or adventure or escape.

I saw her standing, flagging, in the snow. I banged on the window of my truck. She looked up, and the foreman who had begun to hush me grinned instead. There weren't too many women in the camps. I could see her recognize me, a dawning flush that resolved itself into a tentative smile. She'd lost some teeth since I saw her last. But her face was fuller.

She leaned against my window, not quite meeting my eyes.

"Hey-y." Her voice pitched low. It didn't carry well over the diesel sound. "You remember my home country? I haven't been back, how long."

Her words came out in a cloud of steam. I tried to ask her how she was, but her radio sputtered into life. The truck lurched forward, grinding over the gravel road across the sheer, stripped hide of the tundra.

"Hot guts and hair," the man beside me said. "Hot guts and hair. Uh huh!"

I stared him down. I figured I'd find her in the camp. But that night someone lost an arm in a rebar cutter. He lay there singing "Jesus Loves Me," half asleep, the blood soaking into the shop floor, while some guys who'd been in Vietnam tried to hold his arm back into place. With all the talk, I forgot to look for her, and the next day our crew was transferred farther north.

In all the work gangs on the line, you'd've thought I'd still've seen her one more time. But maybe she quit and went back to Fairbanks, or maybe she got fired. The money was so quick, the turnover was almost as fast as the speed at which the line moved forward, cutting across the land to Prudhoe Bay.

≈ ≈ ≈

It was five years before I saw her again. In that time, the Laborers'
Union changed. The work grew less reckless than it had been. I was
invalided out with a spot in my lungs that I never did go get checked
out. My back had blown out, too, and my knees were going. But I
would've been fired soon anyway. The old days were over. The com-
panies had a zero-tolerance policy by then, and driving over fifteen
miles per hour could get you canned. It was a way to pacify the feds,
but the work was mostly over now, too. Trapping was over, too, even
if I'd had the strength, and even fishing seemed too hard to do.

I was down in Anchorage for another test when I saw her on the
crosstown bus. She was sitting across from me. At first I didn't recognize her. She'd put on weight, and she was drunk, talking to some
kids in the back too loudly. They were trying to ignore her. I looked
away, and then I knew it was her. Her voice, at least, sounded the
same.

Outside, the bus passed Spenard, the stretches of bars and pawn
shops. The strip clubs. Dirty snow piled high in empty lots.

I moved my seat so that I sat beside her, and the kids frowned. *Fuck
'em anyway,* I thought. What did they know? She leaned against me
gladly, though I could swear this time she didn't know who I was. Or
maybe nothing could surprise her now.

"Angel," I said. "Remember me?"

She leaned harder on my side. I had to wince.

"Wha' happened?" she said. "That's my boy."

"Fractured rib."

"No, but wha' happened?"

Some kids'd jumped me at the bus stop. I told her that, and she
shook her head. I could smell the still-sweetness of her, over the old
stale smell of the bus and even the liquor.

"Ohhh," she drew out the long syllable, shaking her head. "Take
the pain. You got to take the pain, and say, 'Thank you, Jesus. I'm
alive.' "

I nodded doubtfully. She squeezed my leg. "You got a room?" It
wasn't a come-on. Only a question, for someone maybe in need. "I

been up all night. Just drinking: me, myself, and I. But I got a room. You want to go?"

I shook my head, turned to look out the window. Not away from her, only her hair, spilling over her shoulders streaked with gray, made my throat grow thick with something I couldn't name. What had happened to all of us? What had happened to me?

We turned onto another street. The last stop before mine. I'd failed to love her, failed to understand. And in the end, she tried to comfort me.

"Hold me," I said. "Just hold me." I put my arm around her shoulders, in a hug that would've meant something once. But the time was gone when we could have saved each other.

# DUTCH HARBOR, NEW YEAR'S EVE

Long after dark, they got the last crab pot strapped down. Jim climbed over the load, dragging his leg, checking the lashings that held the stack. Looking for something more to tell the boys to do, though it was dark already, the deck slick with sleet, and more rain and snow falling on the wind that rolled in off the Bering Sea.

The lights of town pricked through the night. The red and blue lights of the Unisea Bar.

"Fucking New Year's Eve. Fuck," one said.

Jim didn't answer. Music drifted over the water, from where the crabbers lay rafted up. Big boats like factories that diminished his own.

"Season ain't even open for three days," the other said. What were their names? They all looked much the same in their greasy sweatshirts and chunky bodies, the permanent deckhands of the world. He never hired the good ones, the workers or the college kids. He got the ones the other men rejected, dumber than a box of smashed assholes.

But there was a latent cheerfulness in their voices; the day was almost over and soon now he'd have to let them go, up to the bar to spend their advances on Jack and Cokes.

"What're you doing tonight?" one said.

Not sure if it was directed at him, Jim let it fall.

The other answered. "Thought I'd try to get laid," and Jim understood they were half-taunting him.

Jim's grin stretched, ugly.

"You're always trying to get laid," he said.

He dropped to the deck.

"All right," he said. "Let's call it a day. Just clean up the tools before you go. I want 'em wiped good, get all that shit off 'em. Last time I came down it was a fucking mess. Fucking I see that again, you're both fired. I want it square at all times, got it?"

They nodded, their faces gone stupid, blank. He saw them catch each other's eyes, backing up, piling the tools together, hastily flogging each with a grease-thick rag.

*What the hell*, he thought. *Give them a job, and what the hell.* He felt a point of rage rise in himself. He choked it back. The tools rang together. The wind wuthered. And suddenly, he was so fucking tired. His fingers cramped and thick with years of cold.

"All right, that's enough," he said. "Get the fuck off."

They clattered up, slamming the boxes back under the table, not thanking him though he stood over them.

"Bye, Skip, see you up there." One twitched a joint out of his too-tight pocket, shaking it from a little tin can. They smoked it quickly, two drags each, before swinging over the side, lead-footed, clever, heading to the bar over the rows of boats and up onto the processor dock. Eyes on the prize, their dirty bodies warm and happy.

"Fucking drinks are fucking expensive now. They jacked the price." Their voices floated back, tattered by the wind.

"What's the name of that hot one again? Sadie? I think she wants me."

"Fuck Sadie. She needs to lose that pot."

"Fucking Sadie's hotter than that chick you screwed. Rug burns on your knees, what the fuck, dude. That chick was fucking prepubescent." Amiably, their voices faded out.

Back at eight, tomorrow. He'd told them that, right?

Last thing, he finished drilling out that bolt that had snapped off inside the gen-set head, a project left for days, completed now. His two hands engulfed the drill. The drill moved forward slowly, a clean line, spraying the misted oil in a hot arc under it, chipping the seized bolt out of the surrounding steel. He moved forward, leaning into it, until, with a whine, the drill spun free. He rocked back, laid down the drill and ran his thumb around the hole. Rubbed his spatulate hands on his thighs to dry the oil and remove the blackened shavings of metal. Wiped his forehead with inside of his arm. Put the drill away, too, and wiped his hands again. That was all. One project done.

He flicked out the lights and disconnected the power. There was a drain somewhere; it was a toss-up whether to leave it on and risk killing the batteries, or leave the bilge pump off overnight. Either way, he'd worry. Either way. He rubbed his hands along his thighs to warm them, and stepped absently toward the rail.

Far off, the voices rose up and died away, tattered on the heavy wind. He looked at the snow. Slid his knee over the rail, slick with new slush, and swung toward the other boat to cross, stepping deck to deck. He'd done it all his life. But somewhere between the motion and the pause, his left foot skidded on the icy deck. He lost his momentum, one leg extended, and caught himself awkwardly against the rail of the far boat, a foot on each, his crotch straddling the widening expanse.

A narrow gap, familiar, formed between the boats. Four feet down, the water, silent, rose and fell, black below the rows of orange and lime green buoys.

The water sucking and rising along the dock.

His first thought was that he was glad no one had seen.

"Goddamn it, Jim, you miserable idiot." He tried to shift his weight, to complete the step across the gulf. The boats moved farther apart, pushed by the wind or by his own body. The gap widened, the lines tied loose against the tide. And suddenly his legs were stretched too far.

"Damn it." Not panicked yet, he tried again to reach back to one deck or the other. But the rail gave him no purchase. He swung forward, lost his balance, lurched, and fell, catching himself with a wrench by his right arm. His feet slipped down the side of the far boat, toed the scupper. He hung facedown over the water, spanning the gap with his own body.

"Shit." The length of his back drooped like a line gone slack. He hung by one arm, wrenching it, trying to haul himself back up and slipping farther down, too weak to complete the motion back to the deck. The boats, like planets, moved apart and sighed, the water in motion lapping up between them.

The water sucking and rising. *The stories we don't tell.*

His feet lost their purchase, skated down the boat. Slowly, his legs slid into the water. His fingers grappled with the rail, the buoy lines. The sea rose to his waist, a blinding, familiar, icy cold. Slid into his boots, his drawers. Sucked higher up his body. Fell.

Chest deep, he got his arms around a buoy and hung there, staring up at the steel side of the boat. It rose above him, high, steep, black, blistered with rust. *Amy Rose.*

"Help!" he shouted. His words disappeared, caught in between the boats. He hung there, waiting, arms locked to the buoy. Its plastic wedged under his chin. Slippery. Spitty. Crusted with wet snow. The cold crept further into his body, fingering his balls, his thighs. The still-working parts; the arthritic bones; the coiled, faintly irritated bowels. His belly drooped, still warm with life. His sweatpants hung loose, dragged down by water, exposing pocked and flabby pale buttocks, now mottled with the lacerating cold.

Death is seldom not humiliating.

Could he swim? But no, he'd never make it up on the dock.

The boats creaked together and apart.

"Hey! Help me."

Again, the tattered, fitful music from the bar. He thought of them lined up at the rail, talking, drinking, smoking, unaware, while this sleepiness crept over him. If they knew he was here, would they come? Or would they say, "That guy was a bastard anyway"? And if he were there in the bar, as he would've been, he would've been sitting among them not speaking, a man widely and vaguely disliked for reasons they could not articulate.

"That guy's a real asshole," they said.

"A hell of a skipper."

"He doesn't care who he fucks over."

But had he been an asshole after all? In his bitter stubbornness, his refusal to be wrong. In his flaming determination to make it work, in the years when men like him were going under.

Twenty years ago, he bought a boat and leased a permit to fish Prince William Sound. That April, he woke up in the harbor to the sound of men talking on the dock, too many of them, too loud for dawn. Even before his mind had fully cleared, he felt the slow seep of knowledge that something was wrong.

He walked out on deck. "What happened?" he said.

The nearest woman turned her angry, tear-swollen face toward him. "Oil spill," she said.

Down the dock, his buddy Fred was firing up his seiner. He passed the slip already going too fast.

"Gonna have a look, see what we can do," he yelled.

Jim called, "Take me with you."

Fred nudged the bow of his seiner in, and Jim rolled in over the bow with the familiarity of long practice.

"What in the hell is going on?" he said.

"The bastards got us."

The tanker *Exxon Valdez* had gone aground on Bligh Reef, in the Sound. Down the dock, more men were firing up their boats, heading for the site, though no company vessels had yet responded, and wouldn't for another twelve hours. And even now they did not know the full extent of the disaster. The mind rejected it all at once. And what he remembered now was how, still a long way from the tanker, they could see that black line on the sea, and the look on men's faces, smoking in the rain. How before they saw the spill, they smelled it. The clean winter air marred with crude-oil fumes, and the heavy, stupid feeling of it all. The brown scum dampening the water ripples.

By nightfall, fishermen were trying to hold a boom around the stricken tanker. He remembered standing dazed on deck, crying as he worked. Birds struggling to fly with oily wings. An otter rubbing at its face. The raw holes where its eyes had been. By the time the company got there, it was too late. The wind had come up, and the slick spread west. Eleven thousand gallons, washing clear to Kodiak.

Back in Cordova the next day, he went up to the union looking for cleanup work. "Give me anything I can do," he said.

"Come back tomorrow," the woman said. "I won't forget you. They're just trying to figure out who they can hire."

He thanked her and walked out. The harbor road was all but deserted. Two men stood talking outside the union office.

"I heard they're not even gonna hire us all."

"They don't have a goddamn clue. We tried and tried to tell 'em this would happen. . . ."

He kept walking, the air still cold with April. In the Anchor, men packed three deep, their faces changed since yesterday. Someone bumped his shoulder, spilling a beer. And suddenly he knew, without any doubt, that the men were not there to drink so much as fight. That anything could set them off. Because there was no one for them to hit except each other.

He swallowed his beer quickly, asked for a shot, and walked down the dock to his boat. It lay, almost ready to fish, but it wouldn't be fishing that spring.

Next day the office called him with a contract. He worked cleanup that summer, hauling boom outside a creek near the hatchery, near a shelf of gravel topped with grass and shooting stars. Every time the tide came up, there he'd be, trying to hold the boom as the black slick bloomed into the shore, crept inward, bubbled underneath their line. Each time he told the story, the same words, "It was a god-awful job. A god-awful job. My crew was ready to lynch me because I wouldn't slow down. I felt if we could just save one beach, it'd be *something*. But we lost it. And that was the end.

"Lot of guys quit working altogether that summer. They'd go home to get away from all of it, but when they got there they would beat their wives. Everything around us was sick and dying. You couldn't care anymore. It was like the whole town had its heart broken."

In August, cleanup came to an end, though most of the oil still lingered in the Sound. He went back to Cordova to fish, silver season of that year. He remembered making sets up Aleganik. The weather dark, it was chilly fishing. He anchored his gear so that it wouldn't drift and sat there as the tide went in and out, catching a few fish, net-marked and old.

That fall, he went down to Seattle. The first night there, he went out drinking. A sweet-faced girl with bright, blue eyes danced on the bar for dollar bills. He tried to catch her eye, but she looked past him at some private horizon.

Late that night, as he was leaving, he saw her come out of a back entrance, trying to hail a cab, her good shoes in a paper bag under her arm. He almost didn't recognize her. It wasn't just the crappy, puffy cheap coat, or the makeup gullied a little around her eyes, but the tiredness and practicality in her face.

"Hey," he said. She nodded tightly. When the first cab passed her up, she started walking. He fell in step beside her. "Lemme walk you through the square at least," he said. "There's a lot of drunks out."

"Thanks," she said. But she warned him off. "I gotta get back before my roommate leaves.

"We trade," she added. "She's got a kid, so I stay there in the mornings while she's at work."

She left him when the second cab pulled over. He let her go, but he was there the next night, too. Thursday. Not many guys came in, and during a break from dancing she came to talk to him. Amy. Over the next three weeks, the two of them blew through his summer wages together. Though it was good for a time, it left him with a hole in his pocket and a feeling the world owed him something still, both for the fishing lost and the oil-spill money lost in bars. Though he tried not to tell her that.

That spring found him walking the docks in Kodiak. He sold his gillnetter for what he owed on it, leased a disused boat, and learned to seine. Amy followed him up when summer came. He remembered running with her through Shelikof Strait, in weather so shitty they thought they would die. Two men sat on the galley bench, holding onto each other and crying. But Amy, his girl Amy, stood beside him looking out the window as if it was nothing, eating a peanut butter sandwich. He never did figure out if she was brave or dumb.

When they got into Kodiak that morning, he was so happy he thought he'd cry. He couldn't wait to tell someone he was alive. That night, he went up to the bar. But in the end he couldn't say it, after all. He couldn't tell that story. He couldn't get it right.

That fall, Amy discovered she was pregnant. He borrowed money from the cannery and bought another boat, the *Amy Rose*, hoping a bigger gamble would pay off.

They didn't have insurance. They lost the kid. She was pregnant again by June. She had the baby that winter, a little premature. Their next daughter was born during the season. He took the day off fishing for the birth. Twelve months later, they had a son. By then, the price of permits was in free fall, and they owed more than they owned. He borrowed from the cannery again, and bought the right to fish out west.

By then, no one wanted to fish near him. He had a name for pushing the edge, working in weather that should've made him quit. Back home, nothing was going right. The baby wasn't growing as it should. When he saw Amy again after six weeks, she left the kids with him that first night back, and went out driving all alone. All night, up and down the unpaved road. He could hear the gravel spray when she went past. Amy. Amy. He sat in the darkened trailer alone and listened to the baby crying in the back.

Two weeks later, he was gone again, making the pollack season out west. But pack ice came early that fall. He kept waiting to fish, thinking of Amy, with a few others too broke or dumb to quit.

*I did my best,* he thought now. *It wasn't easy.* His fingers knotted harder to the rope. *Those fuckers hate me.* But how subtle, how unrecognized, was the fall from grace, the slow turning from the full stream of life into a darker, narrower eddy.

His refusal to talk. His refusal to listen. Had that been cruel? If he'd worked less in those years, would things have been different? But it had seemed so necessary then, to get ahead, to make a place, to keep his boat. To keep them safe.

And how safe were they, after all? From what?

Now life began to run too quickly backward, picking up speed.

What was the point of wondering now?

"Help!" he called, a shout that broke above the wind.

Up in the bar, someone turned his head.

He dragged himself higher up the rope, and slipped again to his initial position. His arms had locked so tightly, he could no longer have let go if he tried, but the strain on them tore at his nerves, a burning pain. He felt the heat of it, the warmth; he felt the pain with a compartment of his mind. He felt the cold. He was still all right, he thought. He could have a second chance, his body not yet wholly damaged by the cold. And if he had that chance, how would he spend it? Still the same way?

The sea rose under him a third time, this time as far as his laboring arms. Stretched out, still hanging on the knot.

"Please help," he called.

Up in the bar, the drinker turned again.

The *Amy Rose*. His boat that he had loved. And if, in later years, the thing he expressed in his cramped lovemaking to his wife, the numbness and solitude he could not share with her, the love and loss that had corroded him so that its existence became his most private self, still the boat was named after her. He thought of her, talked to her, saw her everywhere he went, her bright, neat face at twenty, her hopefulness, her charm, until it seemed she was the truest friend he had.

But she, too, was turning from him when she died. He knew that now, without prevarication. She would've left him if she'd lived. Already, she was worn down at thirty-three, a permanent anxiety pinching her lips.

Of all the things he couldn't bear, that was the worst, the way that life had worn her down. If only he could have told her how he loved her, seen what she needed instead of giving her what he thought she ought to want. Broken the grip of silence and ambition, the envy and the fear of loss that lay at the heart of their marriage, withering it. Lost this nagging love of other people's money, and this parallel love for a barren, diminishing sea.

After she died, he tried to talk to her again. "Hey Amy," he'd say. "How are you now?" But he never heard anything come back. Just the wind and water foaming along the side.

Oh, but he was sick of it all. Sick of the hours, the days, of this imperative to achieve. This lack of capital. Sick of the work, the words, of this slow grind that had worn him down, never quite making it but hanging on, as the boat that he had loved became his cross. And what would they have done if he had failed? Where would they have gone? And all the while, this inchoate, unappeasable yearning for—what? Some other earth, some wider ocean? He'd loved his wife, worked for his boat, and it had all added up to nothing.

The water rose and fell.

"Help!" he cried.

"Did you hear that?" the drinker asked.

"What?" the other said.

The drinker turned his head.

But the shout was too far off and was not repeated. His wife was gone, his daughters far away, and his son too, too hard a fisherman. His boat falling apart. And where would he himself find comfort now?

The water rose, as it had done in summers long ago. As it did, its chill began to fade. He let the glassy warmth break over him.

*Summer on the boat. The water rising and falling. Shark tails drying on the dock by the* Jamie D. *And the men, his crew, working hard then, as he could work as well. The blue-green wind off of the water. And the men that he remembered were his friends, long ago.*

*Summer on the boat. Himself in his skiff where the sea curves in below a scatter of islands golden with seaweed and mussel shells. The sea sucks and whistles against the rock. Rises green under him, heavy with summer.*

*Summer on the boat. Summer in town. A street in Wrangell, a boy playing with a ball, bouncing the ball from one hand to the other. Singing to himself, breathlessly, unevenly.*

"The worms go in, the worms go out, the worms play pinochle on your snout."

*The air over the sea shimmering with heat, melting bluely into a blue distance. Far below, the sound of the parade.*

*Summer on the boat. Summer in town. Those summer nights, dancing in the dark. Because he had loved her, loved her long ago. Half deliberately, he let the ball slip from his hand. It began to roll too quickly down the street, the narrow street that slid from house to house, picking up speed. A yellow ball, grimy with age. He ran after it, and the world broke into motion, dissolving in a kaleidoscope of light. The ball ever so slightly ahead of him, rolling faster, bouncing faster out of sight. He balanced for a moment in the delight of speed.*

*Before he reached the harbor, it had gotten clear away. He stopped, looking out for a sign, something yellow bobbing safely in the glittering sea.*

*A gull sat on a piling, lofted upward at his appearance. The boats rocked and sighed, heavy with the smell of low tide. The harbor crowded, the seiners in. Narrow-foreheaded boats full of men. But all uptown now for the parade.*

*Cautiously, he went down the ramp and walked along looking at them, how they rafted out five deep to the harbor entrance.*

Diana

Princess Leia

Lady Christine

*Algae colored their waterlines green. Their sides were scarred with work, the grind of skiffs against their sides, the marks where one had struck a rock. They smelled of warm wood, mold, brine, and diesel, as his dad had smelled in his oldest memories.*

*The summer waxed. And the fish were thick, thick in the tides that year.*

*The ball bobbed in the water near the float. A yellow ball, smudged gray with age. It rolled lightly, and he knew now it had been beautiful.*

"Help," he cried. But . . .

*It was summer, glittering, running through his hand that loosened on the knot. The chill of memory fell away, the piled-up years. It was all past.*

*Summer. And he was dancing after hours, dancing with the woman who was not yet his wife.*

*"You didn't have to be so nice. I would have liked you anyway."*

*Rain fell on the roof, the music swayed on.*

*All his striving and frustrations were fallen away. And if it had somehow come to this—where, when, and how—let it at least finish with this moment of startling beauty, the two of them dancing unexpectedly, almost after hours, the light dimming overhead.*

*"You didn't have to be so nice. I would have liked you anyway."*

*"Time with you, time with you . . ." the voices mingled, banal, poetic, the words becoming magic in his ears.*

Outside, the others were smoking at the open door, the rain falling faster. And all of it, all of it, was theirs.

# SNOW NIGHT ON THE RICHARDSON

At Paxson she stopped, tired out, short of her destination. She turned the car off and sat listening to the snap of metal cooling, the small creaks as it settled. Markers on the bridge caught the light, the last light as darkness seeped in from the east. In the roadhouse by the gas station, the Budweiser sign flicked on. Snow drifted along the gas pumps and up the stairs leading to the door. The highway split here at the gas station; there was no other reason for this place.

NO MAINTENANCE the sign read on the road leading to Denali. TRAVEL AT YOUR OWN RISK.

221 MILES TO FAIRBANKS the other sign said. There were tire tracks in the snow on the Denali side. People had gone there, but not many.

On the Fairbanks side, the road was open. It led up toward the Alaska range, bent north, and disappeared. A semi truck blared around the curve, its jake brake grinding as it downshifted for the grade. A blast of noise, color, and it was gone. As it passed, a man jumped out of the ditch and ran along briefly in its wake, waving a fist. He stopped, almost out of sight in the light-shocked dark. Turned and shouted something inaudible. His face contorted.

"Mopping and mowing," she thought, a phrase from a nursery

rhyme. He ran toward her. She slammed the car door and started up the steps toward the roadhouse. He stopped when he saw her go, yelling across the road.

"Tell them they can't fuck with me," he cried. "Tell them I'm gone."

She moved faster at the sound of his voice, almost skipping up the stairs to the bar. Inside, she paused, the habit of a lifetime, to kick snow from her shoes before she slammed the door. A habit so familiar it broke through even the numbness that had engulfed her since last week—numbness shattered now and twisted by the blast of cowboy music from the bar.

≈ ≈ ≈

The barmaid waited, watching Laura's approach. Laura had the feeling the woman had been watching ever since she pulled over on the far side of the road in her battered Toyota. "Who is that? Why are they parking there? She doesn't drive well," she imagined her thinking. And Laura looked at her, dipping her head in apology for some behavior she hadn't yet discovered or acknowledged. *I'm sorry, it's me.*

"Come on in," the woman said. "You looking for someone?"

*Is it that obvious?* Laura wondered. "Do you know how the road is north of here?" she said.

"I hear it's bad."

"That's too bad."

Two men sat at the end of the bar watching TV. The debates running up to the election. Their faces were solid, hair over their collars. They looked like men she knew.

"It's bad out," one said. "You got four-wheel drive on your rig?"

"No."

"Well, be careful."

The other leaned in to the screen again. "I just can't figure how a black man could run."

"I hope he wins," the one said. "Hope those fuckers don't assassinate him." They looked at each other, then back at the screen. *There was a time,* she thought, *they would've looked at me.*

"Can I get you a drink?" the barmaid asked. "'If you wait, you'll have a better chance of making it."

"Maybe Coors Light?" It wasn't a place where you'd ask for coffee.

"I got it in a bottle."

"That's fine," she said.

The barmaid set down a napkin, a coaster, and, unfathomably, a plastic swizzle stick, as if moved by a desire to make her welcome. A glass and the bottle, cap ajar. "Cold night," she offered.

She was older than Laura, though she was dressed for work in a low neckline and broad red lipstick. Her eyes were dark, faded, kind; her skin pocked with acne. "Where you headed?"

"I need to get to Cantwell. But if I can't get down the Denali Highway, I might have to go on to Fairbanks tonight, stay there, and drive down in the morning."

"I wouldn't try that highway in the rig you got," one of the men called down, authoritatively. He finished his beer and stood as if to go. She'd thought he was there for the night. It had that feel, a place that no one ever left. But when he reached the door, he only looked out and returned to his seat again.

"People've been turning back. People in four-wheel drive. I wouldn't try it," he said.

"Thanks," she said. "Yeah. I'll take it slow." But on the inside, she was running, and had been ever since the night six nights ago when Emmett had picked up his fork. Laid it down again. Looked at her and said, "I'm sorry, Laura. It's over."

The other man changed the TV channel. *Junkyard Trucker.* Cars crunching into one another.

"That weirdo still out there?" he said.

"Yes, he is," she said.

"Don't go near him. He was in here, earlier. Yelling about something. He's trying to get to Fairbanks," he said.

"Fucking stupid. No one's going to give someone like that a ride," the first man said, his eyes on the screen.

"I wouldn't want to give him a ride," the other answered.

Laura uncapped her beer the rest of the way and poured it in her glass. Ordinarily, she wouldn't've asked for beer, but she'd wanted to fit in here, anywhere. The room was warm, the people solid and real. Coors Light seemed like something you would drink if you were from here and had never left. It shone in her glass, a yellow glow. The bubbles stung the back of her throat, leaving a faintly unpleasant aftertaste. The men were drinking Rainier. Would that have been better?

*Stout,* she thought. That was what Emmett drank. Thick and dark as motor oil. He'd never been past Canada. But there was something about imported beer he liked, that went beyond the flavor. It was a way of setting himself apart. Of saying, I come from here but I'm different. I could've left. I should've left. I could've gone to England.

He'd worked as a mechanic in winter when they needed cash, or else spent hours tinkering with his truck, not out of pleasure but to get it to run. His fingers were often caked with grease, lining the seams of his weather-weary skin. She loved his hands, the look of them. She always had.

The summer she first saw him, in Washington, he was mowing the grass at her father's house. She was reading in the yard. He sat down to apologize for the noise, leaving the machine still idling.

"Whatcha reading?" He touched the book with one big finger.

Half apologetically, as girls did then, she showed the cover. "It's for a class. I want to be a doctor," she said.

"That's good," he said. "That's a good job." It was hot, and the air smelled of fresh-cut grass. He took off his hat, wiped his forehead, and lay back on the uncut lawn, a shirtless kid no older than herself, his body already built for labor. A leaf blew down across his face; he blew it up again, it fell on his mouth once more and he laughed and moved his head away.

That August they fell into what might have been a temporary love, neither of them yet old enough to know. But that fall, she'd found herself pregnant, after some awkward gropings in the car, the kind where she knew she was no longer a virgin but still wasn't quite sure she'd had sex. Because sex was supposed to make you feel like you were flying, and what they did, however eager, hadn't quite. Still, it was a summer to remember, something to warm her heart on in later years, as their partnership acquired its own momentum, independent of desire.

She told him at the drive-in in September.

He took a long drag of his cigarette. "You sure?" he said.

"I'm sure." He was quiet for a while, looking out the window. Then he turned and laid his hand on her belly.

They were married a month later. Afterward, his uncle offered him a place at a crab buyer on Bainbridge Island. She threw up all through the ferry crossing. He, already looking older, harder, bought her seltzer water but counted the change.

After Neva's birth, Laura was hospitalized for weeks. Her hips had been too small to bear a child, and the clinic waited too long to call in help. When she was discharged at last, her baby seemed at first a stranger to her, a small bundle of needs and wants already established as a person in her absence.

Through those first months, Neva would only sleep when Laura walked her, down the quiet streets and out to the beach on the rare days that it was sunny. Or in the packing plant itself, where they could see Emmett. The bubbling tanks amused them both; the wet floors, salt smell, and the forklift squeal. The crabs tumbling slowly over and over in plastic tubs.

"The man in the wilderness said to me, / How many blackberries grow in the sea. / I answered him as I thought good. / As many red herrings as grow in the wood," she sang, dancing Neva up and down to relieve the ache in her own back. Little Neva. That was before she began to show the first signs of her sickness. Or maybe Laura hadn't seen it yet, the bruises on her skin. Her listlessness.

In pictures now, of Neva as a one-year-old, Laura could see it already. But then, she didn't know. It took a stranger to tell her, someone who saw them playing in the park.

"How long has she had those bruises?" she had said. She'd looked at her, as if Laura ought to know.

Laura looked at her baby with new eyes and saw the deep, blue splotches on her arms. Her little legs, still soft with baby fat. That night, she pulled Neva's shirt up to show Emmett, and Neva, understanding something was wrong, began to cry.

"Hush, sugar, hush, it's OK," Laura soothed her. But Emmett's eyes met hers over Neva's head.

The soonest appointment they could get was for two weeks out. They took her to the hospital in May. What Laura remembered now was the warmth of that morning, almost too beautiful for spring. The puddles in the hospital parking lot, and how Neva tried to step in them. She had just learned to walk by herself. She held out her arm for the doctor, not afraid, not yet. There was still a while before they knew for sure. Leukemia.

After that first visit, the three of them took the skiff and went out on the water. Below the boat, in a little cove, they saw a crab walking along the sea floor. Near neutral buoyancy, it moved like a dancer in the water. Each touch of a leg to the bottom sent it tumbling gently up through the shallows, a part of the morning, of the stillness and clear water. A part, somehow. Of each of them.

"Cyab," Neva said. It was her first word.

Later, after Neva died, they left the island and moved up north up to Thompsen's Bay. Few people there even knew they'd had a daughter. They settled in to a pattern of life, one that sometimes seemed too empty, silent; and if Laura thought there might have been more, a life lived more completely somewhere else, she tried not to speak of it.

Until last spring, when suddenly, long after she'd given up the thought, she found herself pregnant a second time. She'd been so happy. That was the thing. A liquid happiness almost unmarred by fear. She walked home from the clinic—it was April—with a feeling as if she suddenly could blossom. "Keep it secret," she thought, "keep it for yourself," this sudden, strange primordial delight. But when Emmett came in, she told him at the door.

"A girl," he said. "It will be a girl." He leaned on the door, eyes lighting up, at an urge put aside for her sake, now gratified at last.

≈ ≈ ≈

She finished her drink. It'd ended, of course. She lost the baby. It wasn't only the loss, but the way they'd each turned aside into their private grief. After a while they no longer held each other, and soon enough, they lived as strangers, the space between them in the bed too carefully calibrated for love. She thought now it wasn't her, only a sadness he couldn't share for a failure that had implicated both.

≈ ≈ ≈

Now one of the men at the end had left. The barmaid drifted down the bar to stand behind the other man, watching the tube. Her hand rested on his shoulder in a gesture that could've been merely friendly or could've been more. What was their relationship? Laura wondered. Probably not lovers, though if the barmaid worked most nights, it was more than possible her boyfriend came here, too. If she had one—she might also be the only single woman in the area. Maybe it was just that most nights, that man was here, and most nights she was, too, and over the years they'd forged a bond that was enduringly familiar and yet could shatter in a moment if something happened. The essence of such friendships was their dailiness. It was what they offered—all they offered. If for some reason, he didn't come in; if he got another job, or she did, they wouldn't write. In a year or two, they might not even remember each other's names.

The barmaid relinquished her grasp with a last squeeze of her hand and came down the bar when she saw Laura's glass was empty.

"Dale says you oughta stay," she said. "He says you're nuts, out there in that rig, on these roads. You got chains, at least?"

"I've got everything." Laura said. "Warm clothes, a jack."

"We got rooms here, you know. I think it's eighty for a single. I could ask." The woman looked at her. "I ain't trying to be nosy. Just hate to see you wind up in a ditch."

"Thanks for that," Laura said. She rubbed her swizzle stick against the glass. "Could I get another? Maybe rum and Diet Coke this time?" It was good to let go a little while.

The waitress raised her eyebrows. Took the glass. When she

reached to take the swizzle stick, though, Laura pulled it back. "I'll keep that," she said. Methodically, she began to crack it into pieces. Emmett couldn't sit without fiddling with things. He couldn't talk unless his hands were moving. By the time they left a diner, their table would be strewn with mashed sugar packets, fingered silverware, and shreds of napkin.

"I know these roads," Laura said. "At least to Fairbanks."

"That where you're headed?"

"No. My husband's in Cantwell." Laura was becoming lightly drunk, even after just one beer. "He took off last week. I guess that's where he went."

"No shit," the barmaid said. She set the glass before Laura. "Hope everything's all right."

"Oh, yes," Laura said. "It'll be fine." This new drink was better—punchingly sweet, with the sharp, familiar flavor of Coke and the sugary rum.

"Well, just as long as everything's all right." The barmaid set an ashtray next to Laura though she wasn't smoking, and, after a moment, hesitantly leaned on the bar. Laura seemed to make her uncomfortable. Like she might need a friend. "My name's Delia," she said, confidentially. "That's my man, Dale, at the end. We've been together six months."

"Pleased to meet you, Delia."

"So you say you're going to Cantwell to meet your guy?"

"It's a surprise. He called last week, and I didn't come. But I figured now would be a good time." She'd sat in the darkened apartment, on the bottomed-out couch she'd meant to replace, while upstairs the neighbor's baby ran back and forth, his small feet thudding on the hollow floor. It was cold. The lightbulbs had burned out one by one, in the nights when she wouldn't turn them out. The phone rang on the little table. Rang. Rang again. Rang.

After a while it stopped. Started again. She picked it up, and heard only the hollow roar of static, as if Emmett were breathing on the other end. "Listen," she said then. "Why don't you come back."

If she wanted to, she could pretend it had been him. That, for a little while, he'd changed his mind. She listened to the dial tone as the plastic surface of the phone grew sticky and damp against her cheek. *Your call cannot be completed. Please hang up and try again.* Then nothing but the sound of space, slipping quickly into make-believe.

"Delia," she said, slurring a little. "And Dale." Laura beamed at her, trying to make contact. "Is this your place?"

"No. I just work here. Owner lives down in Wasilla. We don't see much of him in the wintertime. Not too many people come by once the Denali closes, and the tourists trickle down. Not much snowma-chining down this far. Just the long-haul guys going Valdez to Fair-banks, and they mostly wait until Delta Junction. We don't mind. It gets kind of quiet, but I guess that's why we live out here, right?"

"I guess so," Laura said. "I guess it must be nice." She pictured a dif-ferent Delia now, not the barmaid but the woman going home with Dale. They'd have a small house with carpeted floors and a big TV, in the black-spruce forest not too far away. One of those driveways that occasionally cut off of the highway, up into the mountains. She'd sometimes wondered who lived up there.

"I love the mountains," Delia said. "Came here from Anchorage ten years ago. Never looked back."

"You got kids?" Laura asked.

"Two. One of my girls's ten, the other'n's twelve. The twelve-year-old's living with her dad in Anchorage. My ten-year-old's my joy. She and Dale get along so well. She's learning how to snowmachine this winter. Let her do what the boys do, that's what I say, and Dale agrees with me. Some folks wouldn't."

"That's right," Laura said vaguely. "So where's she go to school?"

"We get the lessons sent in from Anchorage," Delia explained. "We got our own school. But families are moving in. One of these days, we'll have a real school here, too."

"That's good," Laura said. "That's real good." She liked that thought, this little family in the house hunkered at the bottom of the laven-der mountains. Idly, she stirred her drink with the wounded swizzle stick. "I like that."

Outside, the night had gone black dark. Only the faintest tinge of light beyond the panes reflected them endlessly, as if the warm room was repeated through deep space. The drink filled up her veins warmly, filled up her inside that had been empty.

"You got kids?" Delia said.

"No. No kids," she said, though she crossed her fingers.

Delia shook her head. "Sorry to hear it," she began, then stopped abruptly, remembering that might not be what Laura meant. She jerked her head in an indefinite motion that set her hair, frozen in place, stiffly bobbing. "Some people don't," she said.

Dale got up at the sound of their voices and came down the bar. He leaned on it, friendly, looking at her.

"So why'd you need to get to Cantwell so goddamn bad?"

"It's a long story."

Dale nodded. He tapped his empty glass on the bar. "Get me another'n, babe?" he said, and when she put it in front of him, he patted her arm. "Thanks, doll."

Laura looked away, embarrassed to watch. Outside, the promised snow began to fall more heavily now, drifting on the sill. She watched it flash blue in the Bud Light sign.

She thought about the man out in the ditch.

"How'd he get here?" she said aloud, looking back at the circle of light where Dale and Delia sat. Maybe he was off a truck, one of those who thought Alaska would save them.

"God knows." The woman shrugged. "Hope he goes, though. He was in here earlier, making a fuss."

She looked away again. Now that he was gone, she couldn't stop thinking about him, trying to reconstruct a man out of memory. Was he out there somewhere, looking in at them? It must look so warm in here. She shivered suddenly.

"You cold?" Delia asked. "I could turn up the heat."

"No," Laura said. "Goose walked over my grave, I guess."

She sipped the dregs of her drink, and licked the straw as if to make the moment last. She got up to go. "You got a phone?" she asked. But the lines were down. And anyway, she knew what she would find.

"You good to drive?" Delia asked as she made out the check.

"Yes," she said. "You take care now."

"You going to Fairbanks?"

"Yes," she said again. "I'm pretty sure he's gone," she said out loud. And though she spoke mostly to herself, Delia nodded.

"Thanks," Laura said. Delia finished ringing up the tab, took her money, and handed her the change. "You take care now," she said again. "Thanks for stopping by."

She saw them watch her as she stopped by the door, adjusting her hat and coat before going out. The door to the roadhouse swung shut behind her with a small, self-satisfied click, a place of artificial warmth and light where she would not go again.

She crossed the median and fumbled with the door of her car. It bucked in gear, ice cold, the snow blowing from the glass. She began to drive too fast up the highway toward Fairbanks. Behind her, the man had stopped moving. He stood by the roadside, shoulders slumped. Steadily the snow fell, whitening the hills, settling over the houses and the road, covering it all, closing them away. Like a scene in a globe, a child's snow globe.

*Later,* she thought. *It's still not time to cry.*

# LUKE

The night they brought Luke's body back to town, Pete drove out to Orca Cannery to buy a net. He saw the *Arcturus* come into view, a black dot in the golden haze of an April night. It passed Salmo Point, heading for town, taking the shortcut because the tide was high. Its lights were so bright it was difficult to see.

He slowed to watch it coming in. Ahead, a pickup ground to a halt. The girl in the front seat was crying. As he pulled alongside, they stared at each other. A green-eyed girl in a T-shirt lettered FUCK ME. I'M MEXICAN. He didn't know her, but he knew her face from the Reluctant Fisherman.

"You knew Luke, didn't you?" she said.

"Kind of," Pete said. "A while ago. We went to high school together, anyhow."

"Did you hear about what happened?" she said.

"I heard."

"What was it? I mean, what did you hear?"

"Just that the skipper found him in his bunk."

She rolled up the window, her face crumpling. "I don't know why he died," she said.

Pete shifted up. Out at Orca, the cannery loft was deserted. He dug through old gear until he found the right net, and pulled it out onto a tarp. The smell of brine and creosote and winter rain rose up around him. A truck rolled in outside. He heard the rattle of the chain hoist, and a pallet jack. But no one came in.

Sweat poured down his face as he worked. He was thinking of Luke, the summer they first met, skateboarding outside the library, his nimble body folding in a jump as if he could take flight at last. The rumble and grind as he fell to the earth. His shout of exultation. Pete's answering yell.

He shook the net. Let it fall at last, the last fathom out of the bag. He'd flaked all the way through without seeing it.

≈ ≈ ≈

Two nights later, after the wake, the guys started drinking on the shore. They lit a pallet fire before the weather turned. Rain drove against the flames, hissed, and rose up again as steam, leaving the coals half blackened with water. The same green-eyed girl with too-heavy eyeliner stood over the embers, crying.

Pete left the harbor on a falling tide. It was blowing when he dropped the hook behind Grass Island. The outgoing tide hissed over hard, gray sand. Above him, a line of boats marched up the slough, facing the current. A gillnetter he didn't know had taken Luke's set. He watched it as his anchor line came taut, waited to see if his boat would drag, until another gust of rain drove him inside.

Inside, the boat jerked at its line. Water splattered in the window leak. He set the drag alarm and turned down the radio. Listened to the flat, monotonous chatter of the fleet.

"Getting pretty shitty out."

"Yep."

"This is the *Miss Becky* for Trident; we're in Pedall. Give us a holler if you need anything. We got ice and fuel." He flicked it off.

Next morning, he made a low-water set inside the bar for nothing. They killed 'em in Softuk, farther east, but the tide was down and it seemed too shitty out to run that far. He set out by the can in a nasty wind chop and got the line in the wheel on the first try.

"Goddammit. Oh. Goddammit!" he shouted at the sea. "Fuck you, fuck you."

≈ ≈ ≈

Last summer, near the end of May, he'd anchored for a while on the outside beach, the night before the opener began. Luke pulled up on his way east. They side-tied their boats, listened to the slow *thump, thump-thump* as they rocked together in the swell. The water was smooth as silk, a pure, unbreakable blue.

They watched a whale go by on the horizon, its slow progression of breaths. Pete dug through the locker looking for food. "Don'cha eat, Luke?"

"Look on your own boat."

"There's nothing there." He found a half-empty jug of salsa and spilled some out on the hatch covers. "Here." He scooped it into his mouth with a taco shell. "Tastes kinda like chips."

"Kinda." Luke swept up the salsa with quick sweeps of his wrist. He ate like he did everything, like there could never be enough. There'd never been a time he wasn't there, and wouldn't be. Just Luke.

The whale, submerged, left bubbles on the surface where it had been.

≈ ≈ ≈

The fall he and Luke were both nineteen, they took Luke's old skiff out the bar, out Strawberry Entrance into the Gulf. It was a beautiful day. The breakers hissed quietly on the bar. The break was a long one, but they ran straight past the last taint of land and home until they knew by the long glide of the swell that they were in the Pacific. Luke killed the motor just to listen.

They rocked slowly. A flock of birds passed.

"Murrelets," Luke said. He always knew.

The clouds overhead formed torn, white lines. The distant line of white along the beach and all the other blues spilled into one another, the blue of sky and sea and the far-off mountains.

"When we buy our boats," Luke began, because they were both

saving to buy into the gillnet fleet and knew that that was what they'd always do; in class they'd picked out names for their boats. *Sam an' Ella*, Luke's was named, because of how it would sound over the radio. "When we buy our boats . . ."

But suddenly it was too much to bear, the silence and the enormous sea.

"Let's get out of here." Luke pulled the cord, looking for the familiar, rowdy clatter that drowned out thought, preventing panic, preventing doubt.

Nothing happened.

"Fuck." He tried again. "It should be warm." He choked it. Checked the gas. And they were out.

He looked quickly at the bottom of the skiff; saw the gear they'd dropped in for fishing, the Pepsi cans. The slap of brown water in the bilge. No old, red, dented can of extra fuel. He opened his mouth. Pete'd been carrying the fuel. Pete saw in his mind where he'd set the can while adjusting his load, saw it still sitting on the shore. Looked at Luke, the fear building in their eyes. Between them the knowledge they'd gone too far.

Luke looked back at the shore, too far away. Wondered aloud what it felt like to drown.

"We ain't gonna find out," Pete said, to shut him up, but the words were spoken. Pete's own voice fell hollow.

"Think they'll miss us?"

"No."

They weren't expected until night. Pete's parents had gone to Anchorage. He was staying with Luke, and Luke's dad didn't always come home. They looked at the shore. They were drifting out. At the horizon, where the weather would come from, if it came. Again at the floor of the skiff, and at each other.

Pete shifted very slowly in his seat. "I left it," he said. "It's my fault."

"Don't worry about it," Luke said. "It don't matter." He scrabbled in the gear at his feet. Toed out a busted Styrofoam cup. "We might's well bail. Got something we could put over to slow our drift?"

Later, they sat shoulder to shoulder on the bottom boards. Not talking much, only looking at the sea.

"How long do you think it takes?" Pete said.

"I don't know."

"Where do you think we go?"

"I don't think we go anywhere at all."

"Oh," Pete said.

It could've all ended differently. But late in the afternoon, someone just happened to go past, a gillnetter early for the opener. He saw them and realized what was wrong.

"That was thinking," the man said, nodding at the sea anchor they'd rigged from a bundle of gear tied together with line. Holding the gunwale, he dragged them in over the side.

"We'da been all right," Pete said, half joking, giddy with relief.

That night, they walked to Luke's father's lodge in the dark. Got in just before dawn. Luke's dad wasn't there. The two of them went straight up to Luke's bed and slept there together, holding on to each other, without even thinking about it. Two boyish bodies molded in the night, in deep sleep. Only Pete woke up crying in the night, unable to say what he had dreamt. And felt Luke's hand clutch in his hair, holding his head to comfort him. Luke's stale breath whispering, "You're all right." And Luke's hard, live kiss under the blanket. Then two of them, young bodies touching vehemently in the night.

Something they'd never done before, and never would again. Something that Pete now could not stop thinking of.

They woke the next morning, crawled separately out of bed. A distance between them they couldn't break through. When Pete said he'd walk back to town alone, Luke looked relieved. Maybe he was afraid, as Pete was, that they would never be like other men. That this was something more than they could handle. But they never were as close after that night.

Luke started drinking harder that summer. Pete saw less of him. He thought he might've dated other men. But he would never know that, not for sure.

≈ ≈ ≈

That fall after Luke died, a girl came up to see Pete. Rose. He took her to the boat when she got in. It was raining as they went down the dock. She wrapped her wet hair in her sweatshirt, leaned over, and kissed him. He felt her round, pale breasts and springy thighs. But it wasn't as good. It was never as good again. It had none of the clarity of that night with Luke. None of the urgency.

Afterward, she lay back looking at the photo on the wall.

"Who's that?" she said.

"That's Luke. He died last spring."

"Oh," she said. "I'm sorry. Accident?" She rolled over, rubbing his stomach. He thought she meant to comfort him.

"I don't think. But I don't know. It could've been. I guess I'll never know. The autopsy said overdose."

"I see," she said again. "I'm sorry."

But she fell asleep, her back to him, the covers pulled tight around her unformed shoulders. He lay there thinking about what might've been. Rolled over, face into the pillow. Saw Luke so clearly. The slow contraction of his eyes, his hurried smile. The thoughts running, contradicting, in his mind. But he was gone.

*I miss you,* Pete thought, but didn't say aloud. *I just miss you, Luke.*

It was true and would be, and life went on. And it was too late to know how much it mattered, the things they'd never talked about and never would. Already, Luke's face was fading in his mind. He didn't want that, didn't want to be growing old while Luke himself would always be young. Didn't want to lose even this hurt. But it happened that way.

# THOMPSEN'S BAY

I met Jay a second time when I came back to the Bay. I'd walked the harbor road looking at all that'd happened since I'd been gone. The fishing boats looked older than they'd been. I'd heard fishing was dying off, maybe because of the logging, or maybe the logging happened because fishing was already bad and people were broke. But I hadn't known how much had changed.

I was heading home when Jay pulled up behind me, leaned out the empty window frame of his truck, and said hello.

"Eva. We never thought you'd come back." His face was as vividly mobile as I remembered, but I could see the slight puffiness under his eyes, and his hair looked dirty. It was a long time since high school.

"It's only temporary," I said. "I needed a job, and the city hired me. How've you been?"

"OK. Just been living here in the Bay. I tried college up in Fairbanks for a while, but it didn't work out." I nodded, unsurprised. Jay'd been a senior when I was a sophomore, but we'd had math class together. I remembered him sitting at the back of the classroom, all the light gone out of his face as he watched the hands of the clock spin around, his fingers tapping with suppressed energy. Afterward, as I picked up my books at my locker, I'd hear him peel out of the parking lot in that same Ford, gravel spraying, wild to do anything but sit still.

In later years, when he drank he'd go down to the Alaskan Hotel & Bar and ask people to buy his truck. The price was always a beer. The truck was a '77 Ford pickup, so crumpled by blows and rust it looked like a smashed pop can. It had been given to him by his skipper, the last year that fishing was any good.

"It was given to me," Jay would say, hanging onto the bar with an unsteady grin. "But it sure as hell wasn't free. Know what F-O-R-D stands for? Fucking Owner's Really Dumb. So . . . you want to buy a truck?"

No one ever took him up on his offer. I think he would've been furious if they had. The fact the truck still ran was one of the prouder things in his life, a visible symbol that he could do something right. It wasn't the kind of town where things came easily. Life was elsewhere and hard to reach.

"I've been doing some work for Billy Evans, on the *Christmas Star*," Jay went on now. "You need a ride anywhere? I'm heading for the harbor now." I shook my head. He shifted gears and drifted off down the road, calling "Welcome back, sucker" over his shoulder.

≈ ≈ ≈

In August I saw him again. He'd parked on the gravel pad out behind the harbormaster's, and he leaned under the hood, his face bright with sweat. I walked over and stood beside him, watching as his bony body levered in and out of the engine compartment. When he saw me, he straightened up and wiped his hands off with a rag.

"What's happening?" I said.

"Not much," he said. We talked about the weather for a moment before I moved on. Later, I saw him standing drunk on the sidewalk outside the Alaskan.

≈ ≈ ≈

The next night, Jay came by my apartment and asked if I'd go out for a walk.

"Yeah, I guess so," I said, surprised. I turned off the lights and went outside. We walked down the hill onto Main Street in the half dark of a northern night in summer.

"What's up?"

"The land around here is changing so fast," Jay said. "It ain't gonna be the same anymore. Weekend houses going up. Whole islands logged off." He shrugged. "It seems like I just can't bear it. You've got your college and stuff, but for me it's always just been Thompsen's Bay."

We were passing under the bank clock, its numbers shiny through a thin mist of rain. Ten o'clock. As I watched, they changed with an audible *clunk*. A minute after ten. "I should go home," I said. "I work in the morning."

"Sure? I thought maybe we could go somewhere and just talk." He showed me a bottle in his pocket.

"Some other time." I didn't like the look in his eyes. It was too sad, and after all, I hardly knew him. We walked back up the apartment. I said good night outside the building.

"Good night, Eva." The motion sensor light came on as he walked off down the sidewalk, catching him like stage brights. The shoulders of his coat were hunched and dark with rain.

≈ ≈ ≈

After a while you get used to the way that tragedy circulates in a small town. Somebody's kid has a few too many beers and gets killed driving home. Someone else has a heart attack. A few are memorable, like the time Scott Higgins shot his kid while hunting, but most are forgotten quickly, or brought up only as a marker of time: "You remember, it was that summer the Hicks's son drowned off the Grass Island bar." Always, when you hear the story, you realize that you knew the person involved. Maybe you stood next to them at the grocery store the day before, or their kid was in your kid's Scout troop. That's the way it is.

When I heard about Jay, I was standing in line at the bank. I hadn't seen him for a while, and I'd wondered why.

"Too bad about that Andrews kid," one of the tellers said to the woman she was helping.

"What happened?" The woman looked up. She had a bad leg and was trying to balance her cane against the window.

"You didn't hear? Ran his truck off the ferry dock. They found him there this morning—those low tides we've been having—but he'd been there for a couple of days, anyway. Firefighters got him out. They said it was horrible. Crabs must've got him."

"Inside the truck?"

"Window was gone. He must've been pretty drunk not to of gotten out. But he was always a drinker."

"Yes," the woman said. "I tell my boys if they drink and drive I'll kill them myself. I won't wait for them to kill themselves. . . ." The teller looked up and saw me watching them. "Sorry," she said. "I just get caught up. Jay was like a son to me once. It's terrible what happens to kids around here."

"Yes." The woman snapped her purse shut and moved off. "I'll keep him in my prayers."

"You do that. I'll see you, Edie."

I moved up to the window and completed my transaction.

≈ ≈ ≈

Outside, the sun was too hot and bright. I started walking, then, tired, sat down on the bench by the hardware store to rest. I was thinking of Jay as he used to be, the way that sometimes when they print an obituary they'll include a picture of the person as they were at twenty or thirty years old, in their wedding dress or their air force uniform, not the way they looked when they were old and busted up and ready to die. That way you know, somehow, what's been lost both to that person and to you. And I wondered about what might've been.

Jay and I'd dated for a few weeks back in high school, right before I left town. He'd just gotten his truck, and he worked on it all the time, although then it was for fun, not just to keep it going. I remember one day we skipped class together and drove out the highway to the junkyard, looking for parts. It was early spring. Dandelions were just starting to bloom, bright yellow against the brown margins of the road. Ten miles out of town we turned left and bumped over washed-out gravel roads, the secret back entrance to the junkyard. As we got out of the truck we heard gunfire.

"Hey guys, don't shoot, it's us," Jay called. Eight or ten kids appeared at the crest of the hill, carrying .22s. They'd been target practicing on tin cans. When they recognized us, they ran downhill, shouting hello.

"Watch out guys, there's shit everywhere. Septic overflowed!"

"How'n the hell'd'ya find us?"

"Looking for parts?" They walked with us around the hill to the dump. Scores of crushed vehicles piled into heaps, some flattened like tin foil, others still almost whole. Fanning out, the boys scrambled over the piles, smashing glass, kicking in doors, throwing rocks. One kid picked up a length of pipe and started banging on a hood, caving it in. I climbed on top of a stack of crushed cars and picked my way over abandoned ATCO units, their tops lacy with rust, looking on. The junkyard lay below me like a stage. It was raining a little. Off to one side, Jay moved alone among the broken vehicles, looking for usable parts. He lifted hoods, peered inside. Reached to touch where he could not see, feeling with his long-fingered hands for residues of oil or hidden wear.

"Let me know if you see any Ford pickups, Eva," he called. For a moment, his voice hung in the air, perfectly happy.

# THE *VEGA*

Walking in to work in the fall, the wind picked up. He leaned into it, pulled his jacket tight. Bullets of blown rain smacked against his forehead that ached with cold. As he passed the harbor, he saw the water smoke, little cat claws of wind even in the harbor. White spray smacked up beyond the breakwater.

The squall seemed almost visible to him, a ghost made of rain. The boats laid over, creaking as it passed, like old men whinging in bitter weather. Their rigging squeaked and shrilled, the lines complaining. On the lone sailboat at the transient dock, part of the jib flogged against the mast. A man struggled to get it back. It flapped, shook, and finally subsided. The man disappeared. Lucky passed on, his mind running ahead to various things.

Already, the bar was jumpy with music. Men in sweatshirts crowded against the rail, come out of the rain to drink. Lucky shook the water from his eyes and went into the back to change. The cook stood over the stove, burgers lined up three deep along the grill.

"Get your shit together," he said, unnecessarily. "We ain't got time to fart around tonight."

Lucky didn't answer. He buttoned up his shirt where the logo of the mermaid had faded and bled into the surrounding whiteness in the wash. Cheap dye, cheap fabric, it tended to make a light rash around his throat. He pushed his way back to the front.

The barmaid, Terry, stopped him on his second round. She leaned over, breathing in his face. Her bosom skimmed dangerously near her tray of drinks. "That table needs another round."

He nodded and kept on. One thing he hated was the way they ate, the fishermen who came in after work. They sat, legs splayed out, bits of food fallen into the vee-shaped patch between their thighs.

"I about shit myself when the reel shit out on me." "I fucking screamed just like a little girl." Eating too fast, they told their a heroic stories. One talked on two cell phones, one at each ear, while next to him his heavier companion stubbed out a smoke. Voices rose over the din.

"The fucker moved like a raped ape." And then, again, "She was crazier than a shithouse rat."

They were gross to him because they were unromantic, these men who should have been familiars of the sea. He could imagine the ocean as he thought they'd known it, but he hadn't seen it beyond its barnyard edge, the salty scraps of it that washed up against the greedy, muddy, little town.

Sometimes, for a moment, they seemed to touch on gravitas. "I'm a fisherman," they said, as if it were something hard to win, but their stories fell back to the quotidian. *Do they realize,* he thought, *what they've seen? After they leave,* he thought, *I'll have to wipe the chairs.*

He looked out past them at the water when he took their orders. When he stepped outside, the moon rattled overhead like a fragment of glass. Even inside, he could see it flake-white on the water. "Hey, Bull's-eye," they called him. A joke he didn't get. He was tall, his eyes a pale Viking blue. His Adam's apple jiggled up and down like a ball cock.

"Jesus, boy, you look like you're giving head," one of them said, reaching for a napkin, ordering another Crown and Coke and a side of fries.

He wiped the sweat off his fingers with his apron, swallowed his grin. Until that night, he'd asked for deckhand work, but after that, the question was a joke to them.

Up front, Terry stopped him again. "That guy over there is looking for crew. Dave. He was in here earlier. . . ." She pointed to a man sitting at the bar. "I don't know what boat he's got."

He looked where she was looking, and kept on, snaking the glasses out from drinkers' elbows, gathering the plates from vacated tables and swiping each clear of crumbs with his damp rag. No busboys here. Brushing off the crotch-shaped smears on the chairs. He balanced the tub heavily on his hip. When he reached the front, he stopped beside the man.

"You're looking for crew?"

The man looked up. "I am," he said. "Do you have any experience?" His voice was slightly stilted. An older man, with a decent face. He had a newspaper folded beside his plate.

"Not much," Lucky said. The quietness in his voice made Lucky like him. "I could learn," he said. "I've day-sailed back East." Diffidently, he launched his spiel, waiting to see the patience build up in the man's eyes, the way the others listened before saying no, as if to hear him out but not accept him.

Then he realized the man was not a fisherman. Something about the softness of his body, the recent, pink scrapes on his hands, and the clean windbreaker zipped up to his neck told Lucky that. He stopped, already disappointed.

"Not seine crew," the man said. "I'm not a seiner. I just need someone to help me run my boat to California. It's a sailboat," he added. "I'm bringing it down from Kodiak.

"I could use you," he said. "If you're interested. You could come down to the boat and have a look. It's tied up on the transient float."

"You don't have a guy already?" Lucky said.

"No," he said. "My daughter was with me for a while. But she had to leave early. I put her on the plane this morning." A momentary blankness flickered through his eyes. The trip with his daughter hadn't gone as planned. Too little, too late, maybe. It happened. Gone early, anyhow, and the father here.

Lucky began to say something. Changed his mind. He saw the secondary quick flash of concern, the inwardness, in Dave's eyes, the way he paused as if something had touched him or as if he heard his name from far away.

"Can I get you anything?" he said, not sure what else to say. "Water?"

Dave shook his head. "Thanks, but I'm all right." He moved his untouched steak away. Began to talk about the trip he'd planned. He'd sold his practice in Kodiak and bought this boat, something he'd wanted to do for years. "I need someone to San Francisco." Again his voice changed. He leaned back in his chair, speaking quietly. His hands came up, gesticulating as if they too were talking to each other. Limber hands, long and narrow, the skin already faintly marked with age.

Lucky listened until the bell went twice from the kitchen, summoning him. "That's me," he said. He shifted the tub. Dave shook his hand.

"Stop back," he said.

"I will," Lucky said. But by the time he reached the bar again, the man was gone.

"He told me to tell you to come down in the morning," Terry said. "You could still catch him if you try," she looked at the door, picking up his tip, his empty glass. He was passing through it, a tall man, stooped, already looking out into the night. Lucky felt an odd sense of loss.

But he shook his head. "I'll find him in the morning," he said.

"That's good," she said.

≈ ≈ ≈

Next morning early, he went down to the dock. The wind had come down, but the sea was high, still murky with the recent blow. Gulls, released and hungry from the storm, lofted into the brine-smelling sky, high up against a white-gray overcast.

The tide swelled under them, incoming, moving past the dock still dark and wet with recent rain. Drifts of gray matter blurred its surface. Wind clicked in the rigging of the boats. The air smelled of diesel, tar, and mold.

Dave was already standing on the deck, looking at the sky, the sea. "I'm glad you made it," he said.

He showed Lucky the deck, the sails and outdrive. Took him inside. Showed him the galley and the bunk where he could sleep. Lucky stood listening to him, his eyes traveling around the neat, almost monkish cabin. Photographs hung on the walls. There was a dark-haired girl in most of them; Dave's daughter he assumed at the time, but then Dave pointed out another photo of the girl who was his daughter. None of his wife.

Dave stood opening cupboards, filled with food in cartons, never opened. "I like to be prepared," he said. "If you're game"—the hope showed through—"I'd like to leave today. There's a weather window. . . ."

Lucky, too, had listened to the forecast, had heard the men talking on the street. "All right," he said, at last. "I ain't got much here."

It didn't take Lucky long to pack his kit. They left that afternoon, after too much talking to men randomly met about their plans, the route, the ocean, and rode the ebb out to the entrance. Past Hawkins Island, past the canneries, past town. Dave had him take a photo on his cell as they left the harbor, the land falling behind them, and the white curve of the sail over Dave's face. He tried to look at ease, caught for a moment in a perfect image.

"It's for a friend in California," he said, the sound in his voice as if he'd said *Eden*.

Lucky lined up the frame, stilling the moment out of time. Dave held the pose until the trigger clicked. Looked at Lucky, the smile fading from his eyes. A sudden grayness rose up in his face. His breath whistled lightly.

"Do you mind," he said. "I'd like to lie down."

In half an hour he came back up, helped Lucky furl the sails and start the kicker. "It'll be easier this way," he said.

When evening came, Lucky still steered alone, only slightly more confident than he had been. The sky paled out to a distant horizon;

the vastness of the sea stretched on all sides. He clutched the tiller, feeling the depths unstable underfoot; not sure what to do, only trying to do the best he could. Back East, the largest boat he'd been on was a Sailfish, going back and forth along the shore, never out far or in bad weather, only back and forth along the shores of the Chesapeake. This was a different game entirely.

At last he went down to the cabin and found Dave lying on the bench, his hand on his chest.

"I'm fine," Dave said, though he looked too weak to stand.

"I can keep on," Lucky said. "Are you all right?" he asked.

Dave nodded. "I'll be there in a minute."

"You call me if you need me." Lucky went back out on deck. Settled in, sheltered by the cockpit edge. In an hour he came in from the deck to check on Dave.

Dave lay on his back on the galley bench, breathing slowly, his thin cheeks gray, stubbled with frost. His feet had swollen. Tired as he was, Lucky went back out again without waking him. Dave was sick, he knew, but not how sick, and somehow he couldn't bring himself to call on the radio, insist on help. It seemed to trespass on his autonomy, his dignity, as he'd never so trespassed on Lucky's. After all, he was a stranger. And Lucky wasn't sure.

*It's his right,* he thought. *To take his own risks. To believe he's young.* Though somehow, Dave seemed to him like a man who fell in love with the moon and drowned trying to embrace its reflection on the water.

*I'll get him to California,* he thought, later. *I'll get us both there.* Already perhaps he'd gained too trenchant a confidence, not even knowing what he didn't know. But there was space for all these thoughts and more, time for a lifetime of reflection in the wide, unending pattern of the sea.

*Just one more hour,* he thought. *I don't want to stress him.* Again, he thought of Dave lying there, his breath puffing slowly in and out, flat on his back by the galley table. He wouldn't lie in his bunk, as if it could somehow help Lucky for him to be there. To be near. As if that was what skippers did.

When he woke, he thanked Lucky. "Get some rest now," he said. He didn't apologize, as if he couldn't admit something was wrong, but the knowledge was implicit in his face. His body wasn't enough any longer. Maybe it never had been. But he wouldn't acknowledge failure, all the same.

It didn't occur to Lucky that Dave had put him at risk. Perhaps it didn't occur to Dave, either. They'd fallen too easily into a kind of quietness, a remoteness from each other that was tinged with peace. The next day slipped by, monotonous, out of sight of land. Lucky had to remind himself there'd been a time before he'd known Dave. It seemed as if he'd always been there, a rock against loneliness, a solid presence. And yet he had no real idea where he'd come from, nor did Dave know his own background. His neutral, lonesome, disconnected life back East, his distant parents, or the sweet release of sailing in summer.

"You're picking it up quick," Dave said to him once, and later, "maybe again, someday. We could go down from San Francisco to the south, through the Canal, go sailing in the Gulf of Mexico."

"I'd like that," Lucky said, and it was true.

≈ ≈ ≈

But it was plain to Lucky that for all his quiet certainties, Dave hadn't been out so far before. The boat had the feeling of a dream held too long, past realizing now. And the ocean, even for him, was mostly just a tumbling waste of seas under a flat, gray sky. Lucky had a hard time remembering what he'd expected, but surely it was to have been more glamorous than this?

Two days in, they were far out to sea, crossing the Gulf out of sight of land. Each day dawned on a monotonous horizon, the sea broken only by drifts of seaweed. No birds in sight, just a few gulls forging across a leaden sky. By nightfall, they began to stand their shifts, the direction shown them by the lighted compass. Lucky nodded off to find himself still steering, the taste of metal in his mouth, his face pressed to the rail.

That night the wind shifted to the east. Around ten, the engine choked and died. Lucky pulled up the hatch covers in the cabin. Down in the cramped engine space, he found a fuel filter. He bled that, but when they restarted the engine, it choked again.

"It needs a new filter," Dave said. But when he looked, they had no others. Lucky tried to rinse the old one in clean diesel, but it didn't work. Dave leaned over the engine room, trying to help, until he got dizzy and had to sit back down.

"Lie down," Lucky said. "I want to call a doctor."

Dave said, "No. I know myself. I'll be all right. It's just a touch of weakness."

"All right," Lucky said. "It's up to you." He leaned back into the bilge. For a moment, he simply wanted out of this, but he couldn't get out. He wondered how much Dave's daughter had done, and why she left. But it didn't matter; that was Dave's business, not his own. What mattered was the boat, and the man who had become his responsibility. What in the hell would he do? He couldn't quit, he thought. And at that moment, he felt the beginning pull, the small quiet voice of—what? Honor? Self-reliance?—down inside himself that told him how and why to keep on going.

He straightened up. Finished tightening the unchanged filter, dropped the hatches back on the useless engine, and looked at Dave.

"Can you help me set the sail again?"

It stretched, a brief triangle overhead, shaking in the raw, cold wind. The boat bent slowly to the wind. Lucky had the sense they were no longer in charge. The ocean had them, and would release them when it chose. All he could do was to keep trying in the face of an unknown adversary. Keep on his feet, though he might not succeed.

He found himself talking to the sea. It listened the way a god would listen, indifferent, aware, and all-encompassing.

That night, Dave pulled down the charts. "We'll make for Sitka," he said. "Get this worked out."

≈ ≈ ≈

"Gonna get shittier," Dave said. That morning, the weather came in blurred with interference, from the Coast Guard station in Kodiak. Southwest winds at forty knots, small-craft advisory along the coast, and seas to fifteen feet. "We won't make it out of the Gulf tonight."

"It's all right," he said to Lucky. "This boat's seen weather. She sailed around the Horn before I bought her." But he went around the cabin, making sure that things were squared away. Picking things up. The cups that neither of them had learned to stow away. The books and pens that landed on the floor. And the bowls of cereal that were all Lucky ate, that he kept stacked beside the sink.

"I never saw anyone eat so much cereal," Dave said as an afterthought, but there was no criticism in his words. He did not seem to notice enough to care. But Lucky noticed he'd taken down the photos that had been pinned against the cabin wall. He wondered if it was to hide them or to protect them from the damp.

There was a quietness, a not-asking in Dave's face, and a kind of weariness that dragged his shoulders down. Yet he didn't seem now to be in pain.

"It'll be all right," Dave said with certainty.

≈ ≈ ≈

By nightfall, the sky had darkened. The weather was coming from the southwest, a dense bank of cloud that spread up against a sky momentarily clear overhead. Briefly, the sea was beautiful to Lucky. Petrels skimmed the waves off their bow, sooty birds lifting with the beauty and the grace of their great cousins, the albatross he'd never seen. A porpoise rode the wake briefly, flashed, and dove; and the white arc of their sail seemed to catch the light, holding it, as if the light itself was driving them on before the quick, cold fingers of the wind could reach their boat.

The sky turned liquid blue, then rose and gold. The cockpit swayed and balanced above the seas.

The wind came lightly, humming gently in their lines. It struck them with a promise of more to come, breathed hard, died away. Struck Lucky, standing. He'd never felt more alive.

Lucky remembered one night at the bar, the men talking. They'd come in late and numbed that opener, but none of them seemed to want to go home.

"It went from nothing to sixty just like that."

"In five minutes, I was in a four-foot chop."

"I could see that fucking wind coming; almost cut my net in half to get it back."

"Mike was at Koke, he called to tell me, get the fuck inside the bar." And all of them waited as if for a message while the wind flattened against the bar window, and one by one the lights of the last boats crept within the breakwater, home.

≈ ≈ ≈

The water darkened. The surface beat into a froth, fracturing into capillary waves. Built in ridges veined with wind, torn by the gusts that beat against the boat. The sea deepened into a hard-driven chop, and the boat lay over, flattened by the wind. Behind the wind chop came the swell, long drawn-out mountains of water. The boat rose and fell, pitching sideways as it swiveled on each crest.

Lucky held onto the wheel as if it was alive. The boat quickening, laid over by the blow, suddenly almost beyond his power to steer.

"Dave," he called. Dave tried to shout, but his words shattered away. He put his lips to Lucky's ear.

"Hang on," he shouted. He hauled on the furling line, reefing the main. Lashing it tight. The jib had been down since the morning. He slid his cold, bare hand along the tiller, covering Lucky's. The water sluiced over them both.

Lucky slid back, leaving the tiller in Dave's hands. It wrenched from Dave's grasp. He clutched for it, but his hands no longer closed tightly enough. His body was too weak. Lucky grabbed it again. Dave backed away and crouched in the cockpit, his eyes on the sail that thrummed, too loud for speech, rattling in the wind that spilled from the canvas. The swell was coming from behind them now, tossing them forward so that at the crest they seemed momentarily to outstrip the wind. A single brief second of calm held them, gasping, poised at an equal speed in the sheltering trough, before, rising to another crest, the wind lifted them, pitched them, battered them down, their bearings lost in a mass of foam.

Lucky hung onto the tiller, spray streaming in his eyes. Each time they lurched over the crest, his body seemed to collapse inside itself. He vomited, and vomited again. The bitter, hot scald tore his throat. Fear rose in the back of his mind. He seemed suspended in a tremendous absence, his body a chaotic, ever-changing sea, equally at risk from the future and from what lay beneath their feet.

At midnight, still riding with the wind, Dave tried again to spell him for a time, bracing himself before grasping the tiller, the reefed sail drum-taut overhead. Lucky lay in the cockpit, rubbing his numb arms, letting the blood seep back into them before he took back over again. Feeling, hour after hour, the long haul south.

"How long is it supposed to blow?"

"God knows . . ." Dave said. He let the words trail off.

Near dawn, the jib flogged free again, tearing from the damaged roller furler. It slammed against a wind that seemed almost solid, a mass of substance. The boat shuddered at the blow.

Lucky shook Dave's arm, slumped against him in the cockpit.

The jib lashing overhead deafened them even over the sound of wind. Dave looked at it, then looked back at the deck.

"I've got to get that in," he said.

Their eyes met. Dave braced his hands against the edge of the cockpit and drew himself up. Edged forward until he had his hand on the mast. Hung there a moment as if assessing things, his face pressed almost to the soaking deck.

Steadily, he pulled his knee up under himself. He looked back at Lucky again. His lips moved.

More quickly now, he tried to stand. He got to his feet, steadying himself, already reaching for the jib. The boat slid sideways. He lost his grip, staggered, and fell. His arm flung up, grasping for the rail, missed it, and vanished in the burying foam.

For a long moment, he was just gone.

The safety line snapped tight. Dave's head rose up, a fathom behind the boat. Hand over hand, he hauled himself forward, the orange of his rain gear shining through the dark. Then he seemed to lose his grip on the line. He fell back again, dragging in the wake, until a following sea threw him forward. Once more, he got a hand on the rail. He tried to boost his body onboard.

But he was too weak. He hung against the side, struggling feebly, then moving with the water only.

Lucky dropped the sheet so that the main flogged loose and the boat tumbled, flotsam on the wind. He scrambled to grab Dave's arm. But he was too heavy, too limp to roll aboard. Again, he tried to raise his leg over the side.

Hanging on the rail, Lucky tried to reach his belt.

The boat rolled to a wave. He lost his balance. And suddenly, he too, was in the water, the breath shocked out of him by the absolute annihilating power of the cold. Submerged, his mind went blank. He caught himself against Dave's body, still lashed to the line, and clutched him solidly chest to chest, dragged after the wallowing boat. Fighting for air as his face ducked under and ducked again. In his mind, nothing but the imperative fact he must get back onto the deck again.

Foot by foot, he pulled himself back against the line. His knee shot up, hooking the rail. He rolled, gasping, into the scupper.

Somehow, he got his hand on the line again. Somewhere inside he heard that still, small, determined voice, goading him on. He dragged Dave forward, until the following sea, the rail half under, tossed him aboard into the cockpit.

Dave wasn't moving. Lucky knelt above him, spitting out seawater. Pushed him facedown like a drunk to see if he would vomit. More water gushed from his half-open mouth. Lucky tried to raise him, but the motion of the boat was too violent. He slumped over again, a heavy load of flesh. Water-sodden, too big to drag. Another wave washed across his face. Lucky heaved him back, positioned his head, and gave him two quick breaths.

"Dave!" he shouted. No response.

He settled into pumping his chest. One. Two. One. Two. Thirty tries—he could not remember the number—One. Two. One. Two. His arms buckled with the strain, and the numb weight of his own flesh pulled him down over the mass of Dave's body. He couldn't tell if Dave had stirred or not. He rocked in the scupper, his body liquid.

Two more rescue breaths, half drowning at a shock of spray. Lucky kept on pumping.

A third time, he pressed his wet lips to Dave's, touching his faintly rancid breath. The teeth unexpectedly clicking against his own, hard and slippery as stones.

After a while, Dave's eyes came partly open. They pooled full of rain and salt. He did not blink. When Lucky saw that, he knew that he was dead, but he kept on anyway, trying to restart the flagging engine of his heart, as if there might be something still to save.

After an hour, he finally thought to call, "Mayday."

≈ ≈ ≈

Three days later, back in Cordova, he walked down to the slip where Dave had been. A puker had tied up in the slip. The tide was coming in, dulled with salt. The float rubbed up and down against the pilings, greasy with the leached-off chemicals of the fleet, the diesel spills, hydraulic oil, and bottom paint. Barnacles clung and crushed against the wood. He stopped to watch, feeling the difference between now and how it was when he had first walked the docks and even the raw air seemed full of possibility. Feeling the absoluteness of time gone.

He stood, his feet jammed under the bull rail, looking at the flaccid surface of the water. He felt that if he could picture Dave exactly as he had been, sitting at the table, the boat here, time could disappear. It would all still be here: Dave's plans, his stories, his aches and pains, the limits of his body he'd refused to recognize. The way it felt to be him, to bend down, stand up, inhabiting his own particular, flawed, original flesh. But he was gone, and his habits were forgotten.

A sea star crawled a little way. Stopped. And crawled back. Not thinking, only reacting to the tide.

"I have a little place in San Francisco," Dave had said. "You could stay with me when we get in." And later, again, "There's someone I need to see in California." First hopefully, then wistfully, then sad, as the days labored past and their goal seemed ever to recede.

Lucky thought of the girl who looked like Frida Kahlo in the photograph. She stood on the shore, a hibiscus clasped beside her face. Beyond her a blue and shimmering sea.

He squatted down and touched the surface.

≈ ≈ ≈

Later that night, he went in the bar. It was busy still, already dark outside. Terry moved past carrying the drinks. In the shadows of the room, the men crowded up as insubstantial as ghosts, drifted together and passed on. For a while, no seemed to recognize him.

"Hey, how was it?" someone said at last. He was halfway down his Jack and Coke by then, feeling as if his voice had withered in his chest. He looked up, startled, the ice shaking in his glass. Cleared his throat.

"Dave died," he said at last, as if hoping that would cover it, feeling tears, ridiculous now, well in his eyes.

Something in his voice, nervous, important, sad, stilled the men near him temporarily. The bar drew around him then, for once, maybe the only time, its center. He began to talk. But the words wouldn't come. He couldn't tell the story. He couldn't get it right. He knew what he knew, but he could not say it.

≈ ≈ ≈

Later, Ed told it to others. Then, "I heard the kid was still at it when the Coasties came. Five hours, something like that. Took 'em a while to find him, 'cause he didn't know how to give them GPS coordinates. Just working away. He didn't know the man was dead."

"I heard the kicker shit out on 'em," Bliss said. "Heard that's why they didn't make it in."

"That whole boat looked like a fucking piece of shit," his buddy said. "Shouldn't'a let 'em out of the harbor."

"Betcha neither of 'em knew a goddamn thing about boats. Damn fools to go out there," Frank added. "Damn fools. Putting us all at risk." There was a kind of weary kindness in his face. Outside, past the salt-smeared pane of plate glass, the rainwater built up and slid away in little rivulets that broke and disappeared.

# THAT DAY WE WENT DOWN TO CHALKYITSIK

*9:30 a.m. July. Fort Yukon*

A mosquito whined across the room. Stopped. Started again. Sunlight crept across the cabin floor. Outside, some kids were playing stickball already.

Frankie rolled over. Got to his feet. The light poured over the muddy road, drying it out. He let the torn screen door fall shut behind him.

"Frank," the kids yelled. "Hey Frank. How ya doing?"

Frank ignored them. He sat down on the steps. Split the top on a package of Kool-Aid mix, the last thing on his shelf, and ate it with a spoon. Grape—his favorite. The sun beat down, warming his back. A summer wind stirred the leaves of the cottonwood, the long grass, and the four-petaled, rosy fireweed flowers. He could see his snowmachine buried in the weeds. A raven, passing, cawed in the blue sky.

*I'll go to Fairbanks,* he thought, still not moving his head. His hangover hadn't yet quite kicked in. And then, other thoughts, layered but not blending into one another, like different colors of river water.

"Why do guys like me have the ugly glasses? Do they send them out on purpose to the villages?" All his life, he'd had stupid glasses, the kind with squarish, heavy, plastic frames. But it didn't matter.

An ant climbed over the toe of his workboot.

"Gonna go to Fairbanks," he told it.

It climbed a little higher up his boot, onto the edge of his jeans. After a while, the angle grew too steep. It stopped, uncertain what to do. He moved slightly. It fell to the ground, so he stepped on it.

He finished the Kool-Aid in the cup and ran his finger around the Styrofoam edge, picking up the last, faint taste of sweetness. *Grape*, he thought. Next time he'd get berry. He licked it one more time, crumpled it, and dropped it in the oil drum by the step. Stood up, adjusted himself, and moved away, feeling vaguely guilty about the ant.

≈ ≈ ≈

Down by the river, he stopped to look at his skiff. It looked bad. A pile of gear floated aimlessly, nudging the hull. He'd need to bail it soon.

"Hey, Frank," he heard. He turned. On top of the bank, Clarence gestured by his truck. "Gimme a hand? I'm gonna bleed the brakes," he said. "Just need someone to work the pedal." Clarence bent back under the hood, not waiting for a reply. He'd tied his gray hair up in a bandanna. His arms strung tight with muscle under the grease.

"Going good," he said when Frank reached the truck. It wasn't a question exactly.

Frank shrugged. "Not so much."

Clarence grimaced.

"Hop in the truck," he said. "Just ease down slow when I tell you to."

"I know how to bleed brakes," Frank said. He spit out his piece of grass and climbed into the sun-warmed cab. The seat was vinyl, hot to sit on, ripped up in stiff edges, the stuffing poking through. It smelled of Clarence in there, cigarettes and mold. Frank frowned.

"You can push down anytime," Clarence called.

Frank depressed the pedal.

Then waited, settled in the seat. Long time ago, he and Clarence were close. It was Clarence who showed him how to trap, and Clarence who took him riding that day on his Polaris up the Porcupine and Black to Chalkyitsik. Clarence was kind of legend for a while. But he quit going out on the river, spent a few years drinking in town. The glow wore off.

"I'm going trapping." Frank said. "Like that day we went."

"Push down," Clarence said. And in a moment, "Let up.

"It's July," he added.

"Do it the right way," Frank said, and as he said it, it seemed true. "Haul stuff out now, get set up. Make a little cash this winter."

Clarence didn't say anything. Frank looked at him.

"You know how?" Clarence said.

"You taught me."

"I didn't teach you shit. I should've, though." Clarence set down his wrench. "That's it," he said.

Frank walked off without saying good-bye.

Downtown again, he went into the store and asked for credit. Darla grumbled but let him have it. Mostly, maybe, she couldn't say no. She knew he didn't have much choice.

"You better pay me," she said, watching him load up. When he put his groceries on the counter, she sorted through, deciding what he needed and didn't need.

"I gotta have smokes," he protested. She looked at him. And broke the carton open, giving him one pack.

"Thanks," he didn't say. He went out, angry because he was ashamed. She could've been nicer about it, he thought, though at the same time that other current of thought kept running along, watching him do what he did. "You know no one else would've done that much," it said.

*11:00 a.m. August. Fort Yukon*
Clarence was still working on his truck. He'd moved backward, though. Two of the wheels were off again. It was on blocks. "Thought I'd do the front U-joints while I had her tore up," he said when Frank walked by. "No sense doing a half-assed job."

Frank shrugged. He didn't know why Clarence wanted a truck anyhow. There wasn't anywhere to go. But maybe Clarence'd figured that out, too.

"You're gonna have to bleed the brakes again," he said.

"That's life," Clarence said. "Say, I thought you were going trapping?"

"I am," Frank said. "Can't go without my boat."

He'd carried the kicker home and laid it out on newspapers on the cabin floor. He got it tore down far enough to see that there was a little impellor swollen up where raw water came in to cool the system. Maybe it froze and busted. He'd have to wait 'til he could rob one off something else. Meantime, he thought, he'd caulk the boat. It was weird, he thought, how many steps it took to get through a day. Just when you thought you had it figured out, something just got you in the ass.

Like Debbie. He guessed he never should have fucked her. He barely could remember it now. But they were both screwed up after Dan died.

Reaching his skiff, he let out a long sigh. He picked his tools up. Put them down.

*2:00 p.m. August. Fort Yukon.*
Up on the bank, Clarence called to him.

"Thought you might like a drink," he said. He had two Cokes with him, cold from the store. He climbed down the bank to Frank, his legs long and straight, though his knees didn't bend right. He sat down on one of the concrete bags. "Take it," he said.

"Thanks." Frank cracked the top open on the Coke.

"Hear you're on the wagon?" Clarence said. He pulled a plastic flask of R&R out of his pocket and made to unscrew the top. But when Frank shook his head, he tucked it away.

"Trying to be," Frank said.

"That 'cause you're going to be a dad?"

The sweet taste of the Coke turned bitter. Frank looked down. "Thing is," he said, "I never wanted kids."

"Shit happens," Clarence said.

"Why?" Frank said, angrily. He spat. "I never had a choice," he said. "She just wants me to be with her. Thinks I can save her from being fat and getting old. Going through the river ice like Danny did."

Clarence watched him. "Are you going to?" he asked.

Frank shook his head.

Clarence watched him steadily, drained the Coke, crushed it in his big hand, and threw it out into the river. It filled with water, but it didn't sink. Frank watched it go, spinning on the surface. There was always a lot of trash downstream from villages.

"I don't know," he said. "People act like I'm a jerk."

Clarence nodded. He stood up. "Figure you'll be around later if I need to bleed the brakes again?"

"Sure," Frank said. He watched Clarence climb back up the bank. *He must be nearly seventy,* he thought. *No more river trips for him.* "Hey, Clarence," he said. "Do you remember the day we went to Chalkyitsik?"

Clarence looked back. "I remember," he said.

"We had a time," he said.

Clarence paused, the wrench already in his hand. "We did," he said.

He turned back to his truck. Frank stood up. It didn't make sense, he thought, any of it. And the background voice in his head said, "You're both just fucked."

"Shut up," he told it, and picked up his caulking gun.

*4:00 p.m. August 30.*

"You going down the river tomorrow?" Clarence said, looking up at Frank as he walked by. He had the wheels back on his rig again. It was off the blocks and running smooth.

"Tomorrow. Yeah," Frank said. "I'm gonna leave first light." He'd fixed his kicker with parts from the dump.

Clarence nodded.

Frank shrugged. "Be good to Debbie, if she comes back around," he said to Clarence, surprising them both.

*6:00 p.m. September 5. Porcupine River.*

Coming around a bend, he saw a beaver on the bank. He shot it four times with his .22. Ran his boat up on the bank, caught and clubbed it as it tried to crawl away.

"Dumb animal," he said, needing to diminish it. As Clarence wouldn't've had to do. Hungry or not, Clarence would'nt've killed it so clumsily. He poked it gently with his foot. "Sorry, guy," he said, since no one could hear. He felt like crying, but he didn't know how.

*September 10. The Porcupine.*
Frank sat in the bottom of the boat, run up on a sandbar he hadn't known was there. The river was so silty through here, he couldn't tell what lay beneath the surface. And even that might not have mattered so much, but like a fool, he'd had the unit locked and now his outboard was fucked. When he put it in reverse, the motor just whined.

*I could get it off the bank,* he thought. But he'd have to go to town to repair it. And how would he find the parts this time? It was a trap, with no way out. Maybe it was fate, he thought. Maybe he was supposed to go back home. And the whole time that other voice was telling him, "See, you'll never really get away."

"It's what you should do," his own voice said inside his head.

*But I didn't want all this,* he thought. It sounded weak, even to him.

It was getting darker. Night birds starting to come out, gray owl hooting in the dusk. Three notes, each one distinct and spaced. And maybe things with Debbie would work out. Thinking of her, he felt some kind of happy.

He got out of the boat, testing the bottom carefully. If he stepped onto it, would he sink? Or could it take his weight? It settled sullenly beneath his feet, a loose emulsion of earth and water. But it held him long enough to try. He shoved the boat off and drifted downstream, turning slowly back to town.

Sometimes that's all it takes to change a life.

*9:30 a.m. July. Fort Yukon.*
Frank finished his Kool-Aid. Bit the edge of the Styrofoam cup and got a mouthful of plastic crumbles mixed with sweetness.

"Do you remember that day we went up to Chalkyitsik?" he said out loud. But no one answered. Clarence had been dead since last year. They'd found him in his cabin. He'd been alone.

Frank crushed his cup. Tossed it in the trash. But he sat a little longer, not wanting to go home. Waiting for something—he didn't know what. He was careful not to think about her, or anyone else. Because Debbie was gone, and his son, gone to Anchorage last year, leaving him behind. Because there was no one waiting for him now, and nothing was the way that it should be, he sat remembering.

The day they went to Chalkyitsik, they left the house at dawn. It'd been a clear day, perfect. The shadows of the trees bright blue on snow. The noon light red and gold in its winter angle. It was so cold it hurt to breathe.

Clarence had stopped twice to show him tracks, how animals came down out of the watercourse drainages to walk along the creek banks in the snow. The splay-toed, looping shuffle of a wolverine. The broad tracks of a wolf running solo, pausing in places where the ice had fallen into the creek and the stony bottom showed through clear water. The gaps in the creek ice were three feet thick. Elsewhere, overflow choked the willows, thick and slippery, yellow-green and gold.

"The roots of things, they turn it that color. Always gotta watch for overflow ice. Water on it can make you suffer." Frank watched him, nodding, trying to absorb each bit of it. Some day, he thought, he'd do this, too.

Overhead, a raven bellied through the sky. The light was fading quickly from high noon, in gold and red and lavender as bright as glass. The days were short out here in January.

"It's a good way to live, out on the river. A good way. The old way," Clarence said. He climbed back on the sled, a big man, strong against the cold. Frank wrapped his arms around his back, in his solid Carhartt coat. "It's a good way," he thought, storing it up. "The old way." It seemed to him that it would last forever.

# DANIEL, KODIAK

In August it rained for a whole month, a green coastal rain washing the bare hills, denting the sea, stirring the waves of grass into startled motion and finally beating them flat in sheer exhaustion. The river filled and rose over its banks. Our drinking water grew dark with mud. The rain poured down on the tin roof of the shed where we were housed, hammering it, a steady sound as persistent as the sound of making love, rattled the gutters, gushed from the gutters, and finally, when the winds came, tore down the fence.

Daniel arrived before the storm began. I went outside when I heard the plane; but by the time I reached the shore, it had pulled away, leaving only a small pile of gear. Boxes of commodities sent by the state. And Daniel.

He looked younger than me. A nineteen-year-old, not grown to his full height, with a silent, wary expression. He wore a bright, red T-shirt lettered animal. It had a Goodwill look to it, the cotton pilled, stretched out around his solid, young neck. Unsmiling, he looked up the long, clear, shallow river we were to tend. The green hills stretching out of sight, and the wrinkled water of the bay. Far off, I could still see the retreating plane. There was no one else but us.

He'd never been on the coast before. I'd never had a crew, and anyway I didn't want his help. My husband had left me in the spring, left me without a job—we'd worked together—left me abruptly after ten years, and I'd come to run a weir for Fish and Game, counting fish for the fisheries. Alone, I'd hoped.

For some time, I had been alone. Then the manager in Kodiak told me he was sending me crew, the boyfriend of the boss's daughter, Kay.

"He's green as can be. But you might need him," he said. And here he was.

That first night, we walked back to the shack. He went into his room and closed the door. I sat, disturbed by the presence of another person, by the faint, unwashed smell of him hanging in the room and the sound of his steps scuffing in his room. I'd let the room go almost dark. Only a little light came off the water. I was thinking of the boat Jack and I'd run together, the boat he'd kept when we split. Tears filled my eyes, and the kind of bitterness it was harder and harder not to give in to.

The door swung open and Daniel came back in. He looked around the main room self-consciously. Took the table, too close to me, pushed back the papers, and spread out a stack of notes. He looked at it, then up at me, and I realized he wanted to talk. That the books were meant as an introduction, not a barrier.

"You taking a class?" I said.

"Poli Sci 101," he said. "It's a requirement." He kept looking at me.

"You're from Fairbanks, too, right?" I said.

"Yeah, kinda," he said. "Like, my dad lives there? My mom doesn't." He rocked back in his chair, watching me with wide, blue eyes, the lashes so white his eyes looked naked. It'd been a while since another person looked at me that closely.

"What does he do?" I said, looking for a question.

"He's on disability. He has been my whole life," Daniel said. "He was a truck driver, but, like, he got hurt when he was on layoff? And after that, he couldn't get hired. Because of the insurance. Even though he could still drive."

"I'm sorry," I said.

"It's OK." He shrugged. Opened his mouth to speak but didn't. "Not so much," he said, often. And, "I'm OK."

I noticed words seemed hard for him, as if there was a barrier in his speech. It took a long time to listen to him. But he was only unused to language, not to ideas; it was as if thoughts usually rolled round and 'round in his brain without finding purchase in the outer world.

"It's hard on a guy like my dad," he said, trying again, hesitantly. "He doesn't have much to do. He wants to work. He maybe could work. But he can't find a job. So he sits around the cabin all day. He takes care of my dog. And he watches the news. He's really smart," Daniel's words came faster.

"He knows stuff about the feds that other people don't," Daniel said. "He'd take care of us if he could. But he can't. And it kinda hurts him because he can't." He tried to explain what his dad taught him, that it was good to work. And his own knowing—half knowing— that somehow his dad had been shortchanged.

I remember standing at the stove, tired, wanting to go to bed, with that old dissatisfied feeling of having spoken too much and said too little, thinking, *I haven't talked this much about the meaning of life since I was a freshman.* It was the kind of conversation you have over and over, and then somehow drop. Not an original conversation ever, but necessary as a kind of rite of passage.

I made a move to go, and he said, "Dude, can I, like, tell you something? You're awesome. I never talked to anybody like that before." He blurted it out, staring at me, and I realized that the conversation that had been banal to me—and it was banal—was to him fresh still, and might always be.

I was touched but irritated, too. I was irritated with everything then. I went to bed feeling as if I'd performed a duty, and also that none of this mattered, and I lay there thinking, *We won't be friends.*

≈ ≈ ≈

The second day, he woke at ten. He got up and stood in the kitchen, staring at the shelves. Pulled down a box of Life cereal, another of Oreos, and made a pile of cookies on the table.

A book lay flat before him. *The Art of War.*

"Is that for class?"

"No," he said. "I just like reading it." He pressed his hand on it, as if the feel of it mattered as much to him as the words themselves.

I put my boots and rain gear on. Went out the path past the shed and the half-collapsing outhouse. The rusted-out burn barrel and scrap lumber, wild iris growing through the pile. Down the hill to the river, where the weir set a slight bridge across its flow, and beyond the sea stretched out toward the Gulf.

Daniel caught me before I reached the weir.

"You know how it works?" I said. "It's a fence across the river, with a gate we let the salmon through. We sit there, counting each one."

"For the fisheries?"

"For the fisheries. But no fish are running now. They say it's the lull, it should pick up later in the month, maybe when the weather changes."

"That sounds easy."

"It is," I said. We walked out on the bridge. Four wooden tripods and a row of panels. There were no fish behind the gate.

"I walked the river this morning, too," I said. "There aren't many below here, either."

"How often do we check it?" he asked.

"Every hour or so." I felt suddenly unsure. *I have to find some work for him*, I thought, *besides this round of checking empty water.* Inside, I stood, marker in hand, trying to call up a list of jobs. I wrote them on the whiteboard:

*Clean entryway. Paint trim. Fix outhouse.*


"Just grab any project off the list," I said. "Ask me if you don't know what to do."

He wasn't listening. His mouth had fallen slightly open. I could see he'd needed braces and not been given them. It gave him a childish look.

"Do you like to think about the big picture?" he said.

"What do you mean?"

"Well, like, I don't *know*," he said. "But it seems like everyone just sees things from their own point of view. They don't, like, really think. . . . And I think it's, like, if someone does something wrong to anyone anywhere, it's, like, the same as if they did it to me. Or to my girlfriend."

"Yeah," I said, surprised, working that out. "I do know. You're right. We're all kind of the same that way."

"Yeah," he said. "Exactly."

≈ ≈ ≈

We'd been there a week when the weather broke. The wind began to blow in earnest, and the river rose. When I reached the weir that morning, I cleared it of debris from the higher water and walked back to the cabin, thinking that when I woke Daniel I'd tell him that cleaning the weir would be our project today. I was relieved there was something I could tell him to do.

Inside, the room was cold. I made a second cup of coffee. Daniel got up once I had the stove going. I stood beside it putting on my boots, while he poured cereal into a bowl. He never woke up quickly in the mornings.

Today, though, he looked up at me

"She doesn't like to think about it," he said.

"What's that?"

"The big picture."

I nodded. "What does she look like?" I said.

He stood close to me and flipped out his cell phone, scanning images.

"Got one with clothes on?" I said.

"That's what I'm looking for," he said. He held up the phone and showed me a close-up of a soft cheek and light-brown hair. "This is her."

His face had taken on a kind of glow. I remembered that look on my own face. The thought hurt.

I looked away. He looked at me.

"She's lovely," I said. He seemed pleased.

≈ ≈ ≈

I'd been there too long. And I was startled when I walked back to the weir. The river was turbulent, dark with mud. And there were fish behind it now, the summer run; hundreds of fish, a mass of shadows in the roiling water. I started clearing debris hurriedly, wishing I hadn't lingered at the cabin. As I did, I saw more mats of grass drift down. The water rose quickly up the weir. I worked fast, wondering where Daniel was, until at last I had to run for help.

I shouted for him as I reached the cabin.

"What's up, Boss?" He opened the door.

"The river's flooding."

He pushed past me. Turning back, I saw the top of the weir swamp under, a panel upend and the fish behind it surge free.

I grabbed the weir to stabilize myself. I was afraid for myself, but more afraid for him. He seemed more vulnerable than me. The water flung us at the weir with frightening strength. In places the scour had made deep pits. He passed me, moving deeper in the water, hanging on to my arm to steady me. I was surprised at his determination, but I followed him. We dragged debris off the panels. Dumped sandbags in to hold them down. But the water rose almost visibly. Another panel shot up, forced against the tripods by the weight of water. I grabbed for it. But the weir was disintegrating before us.

"Give me your knife," I yelled. And now that I knew what we had to do, I was elated, full of force. "Let's get it out, or we'll lose it all."

He pushed his knife into my hand. I slashed the restraints that held the first panel down, then grabbed the next, ripping it free. Water burst forward in a smooth, brown wave. Three more. Five more. We cleared the banks.

"I think we won't lose the tripods," I said. "At least we saved the panels."

We stood, realizing our exhaustion. Rain lashed our bodies as the heat of working died away.

"What are you going to tell the office, Boss?" he said.

"I don't know," I said. "There was nothing else we could do."

"They're not going to like it."

"No."

We walked slowly back to the cabin.

In the morning, the sky dawned heavy gray. The river licked the bank, collapsing it. For hours, I tried to get the office on the satellite phone. When I did, I told the manager we'd have to move the weir. There was only one place the river could support it now, about a hundred feet upstream, where the current widened briefly over smooth rock.

"Do what you have to," he said. "I guess." He went back and forth over the air, a nervous man. Daniel sat at the cabin table, his chair cocked back on two legs, listening.

"So let's do it, Boss," he said.

"I was thinking we should wait 'til morning. See if the river drops."

"Why? I mean, like, we have to get it back in."

"I guess we could move the tripods at least," I said slowly. It was five o'clock and I was beat, with a kind of tiredness that came over me often that summer. I told myself it was just in my mind, but it seemed to physically drag me down, as if I was always walking in water.

"We have to do it," he said again. "They're not paying us to sit here."

"All right," I said. I got the tools. A shovel. Hammer and nails.

"Here," he took the heavier load. We trudged downriver to the weir. It was all but dark by the time we reached it. We took the stringers, heavy rails supporting the screens, and piled them on the bank above the weir. Stacked the panels and dragged sandbags off the tripods. Marked the bank with stakes, rigged a line.

"Watch," Daniel said. Buoyed by the force of the flood, he leaned back against the current almost horizontally, walking up the face of the tripod. Leaned back, starting to laugh, his body floating just above disaster, certain he wouldn't fall.

"You idiot," I said. But I tried it, too.

The tripods were almost too heavy to move. We bucked them up-current inch by inch, piled sandbags on, and went back for the rest. Lined them up, dropped the stringers on, and put the panels in place. Drove each into the riverbed, gravel piled along its base. Laid planks for a catwalk. It was full dark before we had the weir fish-tight.

Past midnight, we sat at the kitchen table playing double solitaire, listening to the rain hammering on the roof. The cabin was damp with sodden clothes, and the river was rising again. The water table had grown so saturated that runoff entered the river almost at once.

I slapped the cards together, cheating, losing anyway, and pulled my waders up over my shoulders.

"You know," he said, "you don't have to do everything. Just tell me, and I'll do it for you. You work too hard."

I looked at him, surprised. "What haven't you been doing?"

"Just let me go," he said. "Switch on, switch off."

"That's what we have been doing. And it's my turn," I said.

"I know. But I'll go," he said. "I'll check it quick and go to bed."

I woke again at 3:00 a.m., and felt the cabin empty as a shell. I put my boots on and went after him, trying not to think what might have happened. I found him at the weir, his headlight turned away from me, scooping debris from the panels. I looked down at him, at the water, and the loose grass washing past in heavy mats.

"How long have you been doing this?" I said.

"Since midnight," he said. "I think. It just keeps coming."

"You've been here since I lay down?"

"Yeah," he said. "About. Hey, watch." He turned so that his head-light flicked on shore, catching a pair of eyes that gleamed at us.

"It's a fox," he said. "There's fish behind the weir. The first time I saw it, it really freaked me out." His own face was a pale disk in the light.

"Daniel, if it's this bad, we have to pull the weir again. We can't let it scour out twice."

"Boss, it's OK," he said.

"No," I said. I waded out into the river, too.

That first night, we worked until morning, then slept briefly in our chairs. When I woke, he was standing by the stove, making hot choc-olate. He smiled when our eyes caught.

"So, like, I have to ask," he said. "Did Jack get the big picture?"

"Kind of, sometimes?"

"And was that a problem?"

"Yes."

He nodded. "Ever read the Norse myths?" he turned his back slightly. "They're all right. Because, like, you have to fight after you die in battle, until the gods send you to your real death."

I knew exactly what he meant.

That night and for many nights, we tended the weir, clearing debris off every hour. At night, waiting between our rounds, we sat and talked until we found a language. And after time, his body, working opposite my own, became almost an extension of my body. It was as if, through the exhausting hours, when side by side we grasped tools, the grass, the panels, I felt the pressure of his work in my own hands.

On the tenth morning, the rain began to break. That night the water peaked and the catwalk swept out. We caught the boards, and raised the embankment. But we held the weir, and by late morning, the river began to drop. I thought the worst was over. We'd have some rest.

But that afternoon, I got the news my replacement was coming in two days. I was sorry for once that I was leaving.

"I would've stayed," I said, "if I could have."

"Yeah . . ." he said. "That's how y'are. You're gonna leave me." Somewhere unspoken was the knowledge that it might not be possible for us to be friends again. We were so different, not just in age, but in background. He had Kay. And it can be impossible to reach that closeness again when the circumstances of a friendship are gone.

"That's how I am . . ."

That night we burned old wood down on the shore. We could have slept, but neither of us wanted to. I dragged the wood down on to the shore. He poured waste oil on the lumber. It didn't catch.

"Wait," he said. He spilled on gasoline from the skiff tank.

"Careful," I said. But he lit the match. The wood burst into flame and settled in a steady roar.

We sat down to share a cigarette and watch the fire.

Twice we went to check the weir. The water was still falling. The rain had stopped. Once the gravel shifted, there was a *woof* of sound underground as the waste oil we had poured on finally caught. I leapt to my feet in panic.

"It's just thunder," he said, and laughed.

By dawn the sky was wholly clear. The moon was full, setting in the east. When the sun rose, we were curled up on the shore on stones warmed by the dying fire, too tired and full of talk to sleep.

"Let's swim," I said.

"You want to? Sure?"

We got up, and walked out on the trap. Below, the water slid cold and dark. A trickle of foam built on the surface. I threw my clothes off quickly without looking over, and because I knew if I didn't jump, I'd never do it; I'd look back and wish I'd done it. I dove in and heard a splash as Daniel followed.

That night we sat up late again. The candle fluttered on the table. I played with the flame, dabbing my hands in the bright liquid wax, feeling the light burn, the too-much heat; still I was drawn back to it again.

"Why'd you do that?"

"It makes me feel alive."

He nodded as if it made sense. I thought, *I love that about him.* You could say anything, from your deepest self, and he would listen and respond.

The darkest part of the night pooled around us. The air had grown chill with fall.

He sat flexing his hands. We had stopped talking, and I had pulled my hair out of its band.

He got up, awkwardly. "Hey, Boss."

"Yeah."

"You want a back rub? I want to do something with my hands."

"Sure," I said. I did know what he meant. I bent forward in my chair. He moved behind me, pushed my hair over my shoulders and passed his hands up and down my spine, rapidly, inexpertly, his fingers splayed.

We'd never touched each other before. I didn't say anything.

"I feel like I'm pushing you into the table," he said. "You want to move? To my room or the couch?"

I moved to the couch. He tried again.

"Is that all right?"

I looked at him over my shoulder. Nodded. He leaned forward, abruptly covering me, and our lips met, acknowledging something.

He entered me almost immediately. I felt the urgent, rigid motion of his body, its stubbornness as he pounded into me, pumping almost blindly, desperately, for a long time, as if refusing to acknowledge reality. Sweat broke slickly out along his back that was ridged with acne. He avoided my lips. His head and mine banged on the wall.

He finished suddenly and rolled away from me. We lay side by side, heat rising from our bodies. I hoped he would speak first, but he didn't. I searched for something to say. I can't remember what I did say. But when I spoke he stood up, dragged on his clothes, and went out. I heard the outer door click shut.

I stood, rapidly chilling, his sweat still on me, and groped for my own clothes in the dark. Outside, I saw the dim star of his headlamp moving along the shore.

I followed him down to the weir. When he heard my footsteps, he turned off his light. But I could see the bright tip of his cigarette. I walked out to him and stood near him but not too close.

"Could I have a smoke?" I said at last.

He handed me the pack. I took one out and handed back the rest. He tapped his ash into the water. It fled below us, parting above the weir without a ripple.

"If you want," I said. "It could be like this never was."

He didn't answer. He tossed down his cigarette, slipped to the catwalk and walked away. I stood for a long time in the dark. Then suddenly, afraid for him, afraid he'd go away into the grass alone, afraid and sick and ashamed together, I went up to the cabin again.

He was sitting on the porch when I came up, his back to the wall.

"Do you want me to leave you alone?" I said.

"Yes," he said, almost too quietly to hear.

I walked past him and went inside.

After an hour, I went back to the trap. I was cleaning it by feel when I heard his footsteps. He knelt down by me and cleaned it, too, his body once more an extension of my own.

I dumped the last bucket on the pile and stood on the catwalk, looking out to sea, over which it seemed no light would ever come.

He stopped in passing and stood near to me. Not near enough.

"I'm sorry I hurt you," I said.

"I did it, too?" his voice was flat, lifting at the end, containing too much knowledge in the words. A clear, weary judgment of himself. And me.

"It hurt me, too?" I didn't mean to blame, but to share the pain.

"I'm sorry?" he said, softly. He went on into the cabin and sat down at the table. I sat in the chair. There was nowhere else to go. But I couldn't look at him. I thought, *his world has altered, and his idea of himself. He's shocked at what he did, and afraid because he loves Kay.* And I . . . I felt bitterly alone.

Time passed. The clock ticked steadily. There was no other sound at all. I hadn't known a place could be so quiet.

He scraped his chair legs to the floor. "Boss . . . can I go to bed?"

"Yes," I said. How long had it been since we slept? Two days? It didn't seem to matter anymore. "I think . . . at least, I'll be gone when you get up." I thought, *that will be a relief to him.*

He went into his room and closed the door. *That's the end,* I thought. *We won't say good-bye.*

The door clicked open. I turned my head so he wouldn't see my face. He stood there at the sink, brushing his teeth for a long time. It occurred to me he might still want to talk. But I couldn't break the silence again.

Abruptly, he crossed the room and stood in front of me, holding out his hand. I took it and he pulled me up, out of the cabin, down the path.

When we were in complete darkness, he stopped and said, "What did you want from me?"

"I don't know," I said. "I didn't have a plan. I just . . ."

He pulled me farther down onto the shore. "I don't want to lose you," he said. "I just wanted to touch you." He kissed me hard, half smothering me. His lip was like the calyx of a flower.

"I thought you were gone," I said, catching my breath.

"I'm an asshole, but I'm not that much of an asshole," he said.

But deep down we both knew it wouldn't work. And the harder he kissed me, the more clearly we knew.

"I don't want you to just disappear." I didn't have the words I needed. "You know there are people, without them you can't be the same person again . . . but." I was thinking of Kay, and more than that, of our lives, which intersected only at this point. I was much older, more than in years alone and more than bodily.

"You're not making this any easier for me," he said.

He held my head crushed against his shoulder. I felt as if the world was moving too fast, spinning until eventually we'd fly off into darkness. And that would be it for us; that was all there was. The tighter he held me, the faster it turned; and though we spoke, I don't know what we said aside from that one thing: I don't want to lose you.

Next morning, when the plane came, he was still asleep. I left my address on the wall where I used to leave a list of projects. But I didn't wake him. The pilot was in a hurry to get on. He dumped my replacement on the shore. I handed him my gear and climbed in over the wing. He took off and circled back over the cabin. I could see it, a tiny building in the green hills, by a blue river, already receding, already past. I watched until it faded out of sight.

I never saw him again, not as he was. It was a month or two before we both went home. Once that fall he tried to call. I didn't answer. I thought it would be better if I didn't. He had a life to live. I couldn't share it.

Then one night, he crashed his truck out in the mountains not far from where I lived. It went over the embankment and caught fire. He was alive, but bleeding in his brain and burned over most of his body.

I went out to the crash site when I heard the news and walked the woods looking for his dog. It had been in the truck with him. They said that it had gotten out, but no one found it. I thought it might have come back, now that the commotion had died away.

The rain was over, and the day was spent. I saw the place where the truck had burned, cold now and smelling of disaster. The litter of trash, the pages of a half-completed test drifting through the alder. And the trail cut where they dragged him away.

I kept on walking. "He was like a flower," I said aloud. He was.

# THE CREATURES AT THE ABSOLUTE BOTTOM OF THE SEA

It was a sunny morning, and the wind came in off the waterfront, making the stagnant hotel room seem alive. Gulls dipped and swerved over the cannery. Someone must've brought in a load of fish.

"Let's get out of here," Faye said. "Go get some coffee."

Ellis followed her down the stairs, stiff-legged, suddenly shy, into the sunshine. Across the street from the Salty Dawg lay the commercial harbor, and beyond the sea wall, a narrow beach. They bought coffee at a plywood shack.

"You're out early, Faye," the woman said, as she poured their coffee.

Faye nodded. The woman handed the coffees across, black, stingingly bitter in Styrofoam cups. She looked quizzically at the young man beside her but said nothing, dismissing him perhaps. Not the kind of stranger you worried about.

"You come out here a lot?" Ellis asked.

"Most mornings," Faye said. "Before I go inside for the day."

"Where do you work?"

"Nowhere now. I told you." Faye tried to speak cheerfully. "Thanks for looking after me last night."

"You seemed upset."

"Well, I was. I hated that job, but still . . ." She began to tell about the rest of it. How it wasn't the money so much as the weight of days.

Ellis nodded. "Hey, look, can we sit down?" he said at last. "It's hard walking in the sand." He lowered himself carefully to a rock. The tide was in, and the beach had become a narrow thread against the sea, edged with pale sand and fringed with clumps of dark, green grass, the stiff, sharp kind that could withstand saltwater. Chocolate lilies bloomed farther in. Blue lupine.

"My sister and I used to have contests to see who could find the stalk with the most flowers," Faye offered, pointing at the lilies. "People used to eat them around here. The bulbs are starchy. That lupine is poisonous, though. And so's the hemlock." She pointed at the big, pale umbels dusty-colored in the morning sun. "I don't know, though. Nobody seems to know that stuff these days."

"I'd rather look at birds," Ellis said. "Or that boat. Things going places." Out past the breakwater, a fishing boat headed for Salmo Point. Though the water seemed glassy closer in, they could see the spray of white as its bow struck each incoming wave. The sound of it hung in the cool, bright air.

"It'll be hot later," Faye said.

"Not like it has been," he said. "Not where I was."

"Where?"

"Basra." And he clarified. "Iraq."

He looked down at his leg. "I lost it there. Spent most of the spring in a hospital, first in Baghdad and then in Germany. God, it was hot there. And the wind never stopped blowing. It'd fill your mouth up with grit. In my unit, we had to ban talking about snow. There were a couple of guys who'd been from Togiak, this little village on the coast. Way out west? They'd talk about the snow and ice and hunting, until it could drive you crazy."

"How'd it happen?" Faye said after a moment. Looking at his leg. She didn't quite know what to say.

"They bombed our jeep while we were traveling. Me and four other guys got hit. I lived; they didn't. One of them was one of the guys from Togiak.

"Seemed like I couldn't stop thinking about him afterward, though we weren't really friends. He was a lot older than I was. But I just kept thinking about him, and how he had to die in the desert like that, when all he wanted was to smell the snow. I don't know, they say those people have a different religion, all full of spirits? And I wondered if his soul or whatever could find its way back home. I worried about that. I mean, what if it was just lost? All these lost spirits wandering around the desert confused—the black guys and the ragheads and guys like me, all of 'em lost and wanting to go home." His fingers worked in the sand.

"And I wondered how it would have been if I'd really gotten killed. I mean, at least I would have known what it was like. Maybe I could've helped that guy get home. I've got a killer sense of direction. I always have—it's the one thing I was born with that I kept."

Faye pulled her knees up to her chest and held them. She gripped a handful of sand and let it slide away, covering her leg briefly. She looked at him. *It's too hot,* she thought. *It's just too hot.*

"You know what I worry about?" she said. "I worry about the ones that are alive." She put her hand on his leg, the living one. It was hard to the touch, and nervous under his jeans. "Listen, you can still do stuff, right?" she said. "I mean, a leg, you can live with that, right?"

"Yeah."

"And you've got your kid?" Suddenly, she remembered the baby pictures and wondered where the woman was. A one-year-old, maybe, in a pink sleep suit. Fuzzy dark hair. Held in arms that belonged to someone out of the frame.

"Yeah," he said. "You know what, though? I've never seen her. Probably never will. When they discharged me, I didn't get on the plane home. I came here instead. It seemed like I couldn't bear it, going home. I didn't miss my girl anymore, it'd been so long, and the guys—well, I didn't want the pity."

"For your leg."

"For my leg. You know, it didn't kill me, but things change." Ellis began chucking stones into the water, one by one, altering the beach. It bothered Faye, but she said nothing. "You ever try to look at someone and imagine what they were like at the absolute best moment of their life? The moment when they fucking peaked?"

"No," she said.

"Well, I do," he said. He went on without waiting for an answer. "And then you think about it, what was yours? And did you know, while it passed, that was what it was? And you didn't. You couldn't. Because that's part of it, that you think then things will keep getting better.

"Just a year ago, I had both legs. Last March I was learning how to surf. I had a thing for it. I picked it up quick. The other guys would talk about that. And I was twenty-one. I was going to be someone. But not long after that, we shipped to Iraq. And all I could do was remember it.

"I used to love it out there, surfing. When you catch a wave, you are so absolutely alive. So perfectly what you are. It's just the sea and you, nothing else matters."

He kicked his good leg. "That's why I couldn't go back. I couldn't've stood it, seeing other guys ride the waves. Because, you know, I can still walk. But I'll never surf like that again. Not quite like that. And it's like my life is over, and I'm still here. I came to Alaska, thinking things would be different. I remembered what that guy from Togiak told me. I thought I'd get here and it would be all right. But it isn't."

Faye watched him, struck. "I know that feeling," she said at last. "But . . . yeah."

"You ever been out there?" He pointed at the water.

"Yeah."

Thinking about it, she decided not to explain. It seemed a stupid story next to his. Instead, her grasp tightened on his leg. She moved her hand up and down. "Can you feel in the other leg, too?" she asked.

"You know, I can. It hurts sometimes," he said.

"Let me touch it," she said. He nodded slowly. Reaching over, she could feel the rigidity of it, unbending and unalive. She worked her fingers up, until she came to flesh again, just below the hip. "I'm amazed you didn't bleed to death," she said bluntly.

"So am I." The scene had blurred together in his mind, as if he'd been drugged, but he did remember seeing his leg and thinking that was it. That was all there was.

She kneaded steadily, not asking now. Her fingers traced his lean belly, and slid under his belt buckle to feel the warm, living thing beneath, and the coarse hair. Slowly, he brought up his hand, shifting his balance, and touched her bare shoulder, smooth, marked in sand, and the drift of her ponytail, so soft it startled him.

Afterward, they lay together in the sand, in the breeze from the still-blue ocean. For a moment, Faye's worry had stilled. She lay with her arms flung out, her eyes half closed.

"What did you say these things were called?" Ellis asked at last, looking at the flowers. Faye shrugged. She didn't feel like talking. Then, regretting it, she said. "I worry . . . I worry about these plants and things. The world's changing too fast."

"You know," he said. "When I was in the hospital in Germany, there was a guy in the next bed. He told me there are creatures under the sea. Way down, where the light doesn't reach, and there's so much pressure it's always cold. No matter what happens up here on the surface, it doesn't change. He must have been some kind of scientist. I never could figure out what he was doing there. But I used to like to think about those creatures. It'd be so cold, down there. You could forget about everything, everything at all."

Faye squinted against the sun, at the blue water. It looked almost metallic now, the waves barbed with light.

"Think about it," he said. "It'll make you feel better. The creatures at the absolute bottom of the sea."